This book should be retu... the
...re Count... wn

THE LAST
MINUTE

www.**davidficklingbooks**.co.uk

Also by Eleanor Updale:

Johnny Swanson

THE LAST
MINUTE

ELEANOR UPDALE

David Fickling Books

OXFORD · NEW YORK
31 Beaumont Street
Oxford OX1 2NP, UK

THE LAST MINUTE
A DAVID FICKLING BOOK 978 0 385 61668 3

Published in Great Britain by David Fickling Books,
a division of Random House Children's Publishers UK
A Random House Group Company

This edition published 2013

1 3 5 7 9 10 8 6 4 2

The Random House Group Limited supports The Forest Stewardship
Council (FSC®), the leading international forest certification organisation.
Our books carrying the FSC label are printed on FSC® certified paper.
FSC is the only forest certification scheme endorsed by the leading
environmental organisations, including Greenpeace. Our
paper procurement policy can be found at
www.randomhouse.co.uk/environment

MIX
Paper from
responsible sources
FSC® C016897

Set in New Baskerville

DAVID FICKLING BOOKS
31 Beaumont Street, Oxford, OX1 2NP

www.randomhousechildrens.co.uk
www.totallyrandombooks.co.uk
www.randomhouse.co.uk

Addresses for companies within The Random House Group Limited can be found at:
www.randomhouse.co.uk/offices.htm

THE RANDOM HOUSE GROUP Limited Reg. No. 954009

A CIP catalogue record for this book is available from the British Library.

Printed and bound in Great Britain by Clays Ltd, St Ives PLC

To Eleonore, Vivian and Maria.
With admiration and thanks.

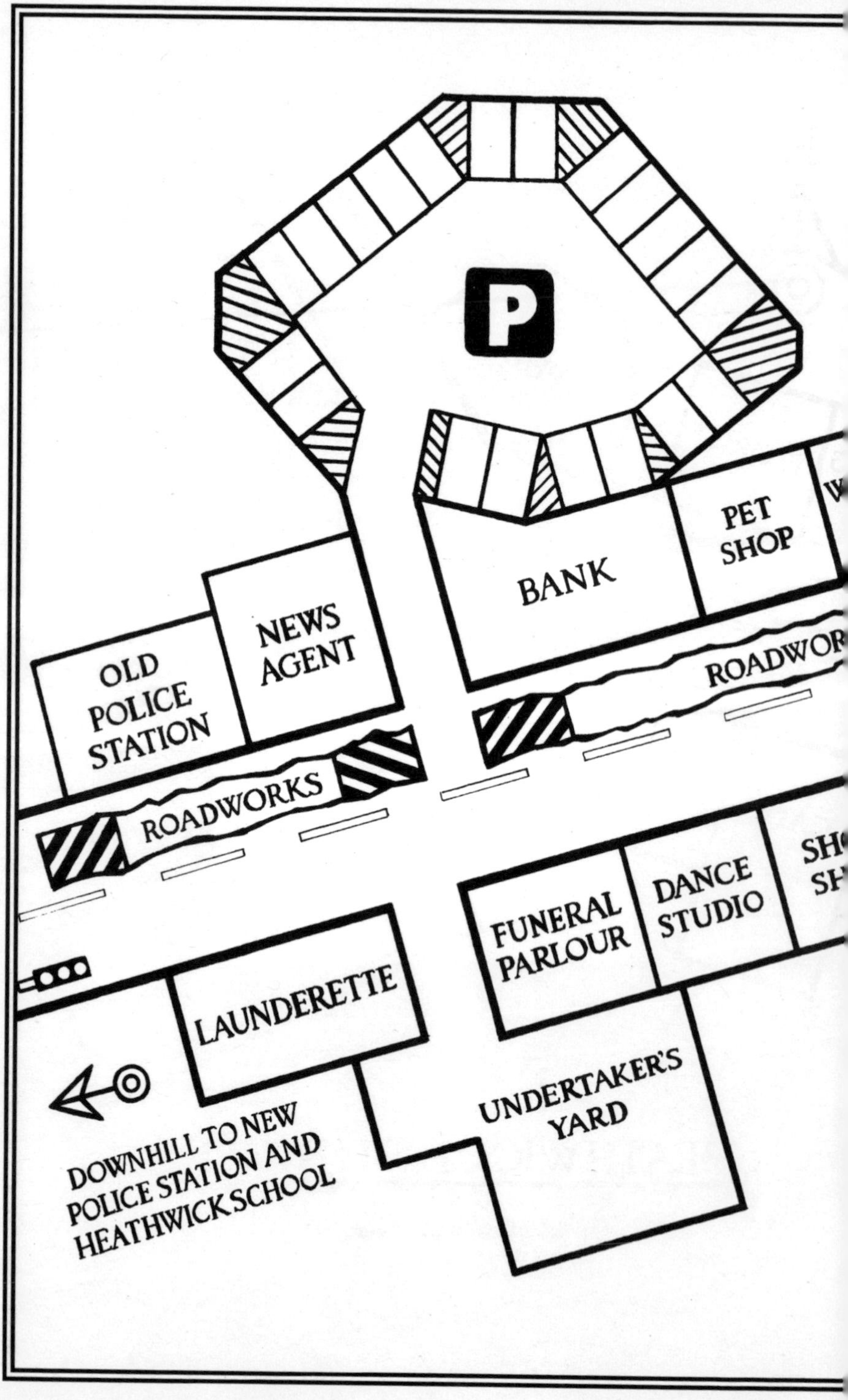

P

OLD
POLICE
STATION

NEWS
AGENT

BANK

PET
SHOP

W

ROADWOR

ROADWORKS

ROADWORKS

FUNERAL
PARLOUR

DANCE
STUDIO

SH
SH

LAUNDERETTE

UNDERTAKER'S
YARD

DOWNHILL TO NEW
POLICE STATION AND
HEATHWICK SCHOOL

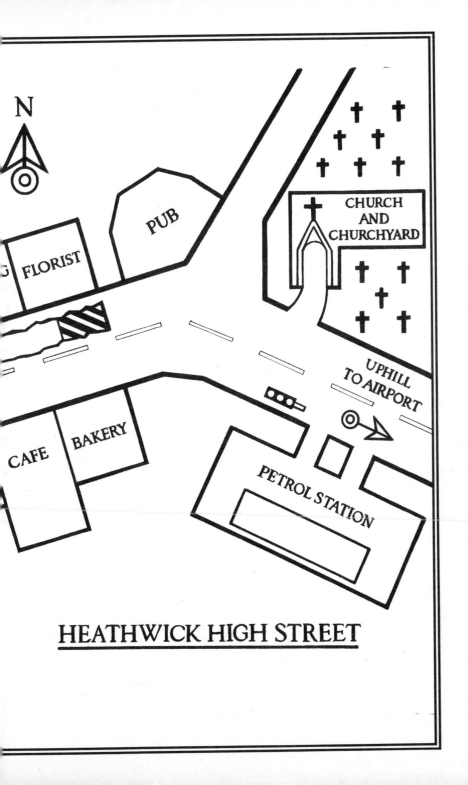

PROLOGUE

9.33 a.m.

Dust. A cold wind. The first shards of icy rain. The front of the shop has dropped away. Underwear and silk stockings wave, indecently, towards the street. A woman in a shredded wedding dress still poses – head tilted proudly, one hand on her hip – but she's bald, and swaying on her mangled stand as if she's had too much to drink at the reception. Metres away, her bridesmaid's plastic arm rises in triumph above the rubble, clutching a posy of synthetic flowers. Another hand – paler, frantic, flecked with gory grime – forces its way between the fallen bricks, grasping for help, but finding only the bride's lost nylon wig, its golden ringlets caked in plaster. Next door and two floors up, an Advent calendar is stuck on the wall, half its windows open to the street. A fireplace clings on in mid-air, with a couple of photographs still balanced on its mantelpiece. A chubby boy in a tight school sweatshirt squints awkwardly towards the camera. A family group stares through a spider's web of shattered glass, their staged unflappability frozen in black and white a century ago. A television dangles upside-down from the plug alongside the grate. Banal chatter bleeds from its speakers onto the catastrophe below:

(*The presenter starts fiddling with his earpiece*) '. . . I'm sorry, Mavis, I'll have to interrupt you a moment, because we have some breaking news coming in. Excuse me while I take a look at my computer. There aren't many details. Unconfirmed – and I must stress, unconfirmed – reports of an explosion in Heathwick High Street . . . We've had a tweet from one of our viewers – Robbie (Thanks for that, Robbie) – saying some buildings have collapsed. Obviously, our newsroom has been on to the police, and for now they're saying only that they're investigating. But they're advising motorists to avoid the Heathwick area for the time being.

(*He looks up again, at the wrong camera*) 'Not very easy, if you're going to the airport. And it was bad enough already with those roadworks Trish the Travel was telling us about earlier. No doubt she'll have an update for us in her regular slot at five to ten, so stick with us for that.

(*Turns to the right camera*) 'To recap: that's unconfirmed reports of an explosion in the vicinity of Heathwick

High Street. And of course we will keep you up to date here, and on the website, as more details come in.

'Now, Mavis. Back to the cake. Exactly how do you make those sugar holly leaves for the decoration?'

TICK

59 seconds to go . . .

9.21 a.m.

High on the hill, Matthew Larkin dips his brush into the pot of red paint he's holding in his other hand. His ladder leans against a hoarding at the front of the churchyard, and from the top he can see right down the High Street sloping away from him. He's seventy-two, and his overalls are loose on his shrinking frame, but after a lifetime as a steeplejack he's comfortable at such a height: secure in his footing, untroubled by the wind, and glad to be away from the pre-Christmas bustle below. It's a mess. Emergency gasworks have closed one side of the street, and traffic in both directions has been trying to cheat the slow temporary lights all morning. The result is gridlock, with two lines of cars facing each other at a standstill as a digger waltzes around between them. In his time, Matthew has been part of many a campaign against widening the road. It's a major bottleneck on the way to the airport, but some of the shops on either side date back centuries, even if the businesses they house have changed. The new coffee bar, halfway down on Matthew's left, is the first, unwelcome, sign of the global chains moving in, and now that the petrol station behind him has been extended to include a section selling groceries, he wonders how long the newsagent down at the bottom on the right can survive.

It's cold, but Matthew is determined to get this job done before he leaves to meet his daughter, who's flying over from New Zealand. They both know that this might be her last visit in his lifetime, though neither has put the thought into words. He doesn't want to be late, or to have any distractions during her stay, so he's painting the sign now. It's a huge chart in the shape of a thermometer, showing how the fundraising for repairs to the church roof is going. Matthew promised the vicar that he would update it regularly, and the latest figures were announced on Sunday: another two thousand pounds, thanks to an auction at the local private school, where the headmaster's brassy American wife bullied the parents into paying large sums for things they didn't want. It will only take a few minutes to top up the red line.

There's another school in Heathwick – not the sort that holds charity auctions, but the place where most of the local children end up. Today, 8C are on a trip. They're in the coach Matthew can see bouncing to a halt halfway along the High Street, between the bank on one side and the new dance studio on the other. On board, the harassed teacher, Miss Hunter, is worrying whether they will reach the city in time for curtain-up on the special performance of *Julius Caesar*, and wishes she had insisted on an earlier start. Her nervous habit of repeatedly tucking her limp, prematurely greying hair behind her ears is more in evidence than usual. She was against giving Year 8 a Christmas treat in the first place. As far as she can see they have done nothing to deserve it, and apart from their joy at getting out of the classroom, none of them shows any sign of wanting to go to the theatre. This has been the most unpleasant term she can remember. Every day has been a struggle, and this one holds new horrors. Miss Hunter is looking ahead to an afternoon of humiliation and embarrassment in front of colleagues from other schools, where the children have somehow learned to behave. She flicks her hair behind her ears yet again.

From the window, she catches sight of Lenny Gibbon, the boy they wasted twenty minutes waiting for at the school gates. Eventually Lenny's mother had phoned the office to say he was ill, but here she is now, dragging him along the High Street. Lenny's pale and tired. It would be charitable to suppose that they are on their way to the doctor's, but Lenny looks like that every day, and they're outside the shoe shop, with Mrs Gibbon making for a rack of cheap lace-ups. It wouldn't surprise Miss Hunter if Lenny had been kept off school just to be taken to the sales.

Lucy Noble, the pregnant woman with the expensive and unwieldy pushchair, is in a hurry. She's on her way to her mother-in-law's house, to drop off her daughter so that she can go to this afternoon's appointment at the clinic by herself. Just a few weeks now, and little Chloe will have a new brother or sister. Lucy knows that the midwife can see from the scans whether it's a boy or a girl, but she's asked not to be told. She's looking forward to the surprise that will await her in the delivery room, thrilled at the prospect of a new family member, what- ever its sex. She's even secretly hoping that the baby might arrive just a little early: a special Christmas child. But even so, this pregnancy is less fun than the last. It's hard work trailing round with a toddler and all the tackle that goes with her when you're enormous and exhausted.

Lucy has already left the newsagent's and struggled past the white van that is blocking the mouth of the car park. As usual, she's ignored the beggar who sits by the cash machine every day half-heartedly asking for change. She's looking for a space where she can get through the roadworks and across the street, when a young man with a large rucksack on his back taps her on the shoulder, and hands her a tiny pink mitten that's fallen to the ground.

Alongside Lucy, a tall, fat man – Bernie Blackstock, manager of the local pub – is looking with despair at the mess his dog, Ritzi, has deposited on the pavement. If the puppy had aimed just a few inches to the left, into the filthy trench of exposed pipes and clay that's being excavated by the noisy digging machines and drills, Bernie wouldn't feel obliged to clean up. But the pretty little girl in the pushchair is pointing excitedly at Ritzi, shouting 'Doggie! Doggie!' and Bernie suspects that her mother may be the source of the bossy sign on the community notice board outside the bank. THERE'S NO SUCH THING AS THE DOG POO FAIRY, it says, reminding dog owners that the microbes lurking in their pets' mess can turn babies blind. Bernie doesn't need that patronizing notice to tell him that he can't risk leaving the glistening brown heap where it is. Anyone could step in it. There are people around who might recognize him and spread news of his antisocial behaviour to potential customers. It doesn't take much to give you a bad name round here, and he can't afford to lose trade. That's the thing about running a pub. You're never off duty – never out of the public eye. But Bernie's got Ritzi's lead in one hand and a letter in the other, so picking up the poo isn't going to be easy. He puts the envelope between his teeth, and rummages for the plastic bag in his pocket. He has no hands free to cover his ears as the brakes of the school coach give a high-pitched pneumatic wheeze.

TOCK

58 seconds to go . . .

Matthew Larkin wipes his brush against the side of his paint tin.

A spotty, skinny youth, wearing an orange jerkin with GIFTFORCE written in purple capitals across the back, has already sidestepped the beggar and the defecating dog. Now, hugging his clipboard and rubbing his hands in the cold, he takes up position a little further along the street: outside the florist's at the corner opposite the churchyard, where the pavement is so narrow that no one will be able to pass him with ease. This is Nicholas Birkham, who was hoping to have more fun on his gap year before medical school. He needs money quickly so he can go off travelling, and the only job he could get was with an agency that raises funds for charities. He has to persuade people to hand over their bank details in the street so that regular payments can be taken from their accounts. This week he's trying to interest shoppers in the plight of the homeless. It's a harder sell than the animal rescue centre he was promoting in November. Nick's used now to the way shoppers cross the street if they spot him in time, so the roadworks are a blessing for him today. The gas company diggers have blocked off that escape route. With a bit of luck, and if the rain holds off, he might reach his target number of sign-ups before it gets dark and even colder. In some ways the time of year is an advantage – some folk are in a giving mood in the run-up to Christmas – but the days are short, and the extra costs of heating and buying presents put a zip on many a purse.

Outside the bank, Bernie gets his free hand inside the plastic bag, and Lucy says a quick 'Thank you' without really looking at the man who gave her the mitten. Chloe, apparently untroubled by the cold, is waving her bare hand and giggling as she repeats, 'Doggie! Doggie!' The cute little puppy, a golden cocker spaniel with glistening brown eyes, beats its tail against the side of the pushchair as it tries to pull Bernie downhill towards the park.

Behind them, in the narrow lane between the newsagent and the bank which forms the exit from the car park, Anthony Dougall (who has been sounding the horn of his top-of-the-range Audi for some time) angrily flings open the door. The driver of the van in front of him has taken no notice of the tooting and the flashing head-lights, and is still blocking the way out onto the main road.

Anthony Dougall is a local councillor, and now a prospective parliamentary candidate. It's his birthday. He's on a tight timetable, and he's not used to having his plans upset. That's just as well because, for the past few months, Anthony has had to plan very carefully. What started as a quick fumble with a young volunteer at his party offices has somehow turned into something more serious, deliciously threatening everything he has schemed for over the years. He wasn't to know that a by-election would arise so soon, before he'd had time to explain everything to his wife, or quietly get rid of his mistress. What bad luck that his big chance was brought about by the disgrace of the sitting MP, caught in a squalid fraud, and that his own wholesomeness would inevitably be part of his party's election pitch. He'd thought Sharon (sweet, naïve Sharon) understood that their relationship didn't really mean anything. But it turned out that it did (to her) and so might for him, politically, whether he likes it or not.

From behind the van, Anthony can't see that the traffic in the main road is static, and hardly worth joining, anyway.

Across the street, opposite the bank, is the long-empty video shop that has now been turned into a dance and exercise studio. Through the plate-glass window the first 'keep fit' class of the day can be seen limbering up. They are mainly mothers fresh from the school run, dressed in everything from pyjama bottoms and sloppy T-shirts to bright, tight leotards. They gossip and chuckle as they roll their shoulders and stretch their calves.

Two doors along, past the shoe shop, in the café that used to be the public library, less athletic parents are queuing for cappuccinos and skinny lattes. Eighteen-year-old Sam Riley, the new trainee – too new to be allowed to serve at the counter alone – is reminding himself that he's lucky to have a job, even though his boss is a stickler for cleanliness, and Sam is having to wield mops and brushes in a way that doesn't come naturally at all. He's a quiet boy, small for his age, and well aware of what a disappointment he is to his parents. They'd expected him to study law, as they had done. Sam did everything asked of him at school, but somehow the grades didn't come. He'd like to be a carpenter, but he knows his father would laugh at the idea of his son doing anything 'manual', and his mother would shriek with social shame. He hasn't dared tell her about the café job. She thinks he's revising for retakes. Sam eases his way between the oversized buggies to collect empty mugs and rearrange chairs, but he's too shy to disturb the earnest group by the window, all dressed in black, who are clearly killing time before a funeral.

Over the car horns and the noise of the diggers, the beggar shouts to Bernie, even though he's just a metre or so away. 'Here, mate!' he bellows, as Janine Nailor, the florist, pushes past, clasping a large wreath of red and white flowers, trying to find a place to cross the road. She's agitated, and her breath turns to vapour as she mumbles to herself about how stupid she's been. She promised to get the wreath to the undertaker by nine, but lost track of time as she sorted out her shop for the day. How could she, when she'd been up half the night weaving the blooms into the wire frame? Of course, that sleepless night may be the reason. Janine aches with tiredness. You'd think making a wreath in the form of a lifebelt would be easy. After all, it's circular – nothing like as much of a challenge as the guitar she'd had to do last month. But she'd found it really difficult to settle to the work, and that was why it had taken her so long. It made her feel uncomfortable. She'd had some pretty tasteless requests before, but a lifebelt for a dead man? Still, it was what the widow wanted, and she'd paid for it. The deceased had been a keen yachtsman, apparently. Janine hadn't liked to ask whether he'd drowned.

She'd gone into floristry to try to get away from the pressures of her office job, and in the hope of having more time to look after her son, Calum, and her demented elderly mother. But it's just as bad – no, worse – working with perishable goods and still up against deadlines like this funeral. In the flat above the shop, her mother, Margaret Sharp, was awake till the small hours, rattling the front door, and crying out about some imagined danger she couldn't explain. Janine had locked her mother in her bedroom for her own safety when she went to the early-morning market to buy today's stock. Then Calum had left it till after breakfast to mention that he needed a packed lunch for the school trip. In the end, Janine hadn't had time to brush her own hair, let alone wash her mother's, before opening the shop for the day.

Now she's hurrying to get the wreath to the funeral parlour before the hearse sets off for the church. She doesn't even look at the beggar as she steps over his feet. The scruffy man is such a feature of the place that she has stopped wondering who he is, or how he came to be there. Everyone refers to him as Matey – no doubt because he calls everybody 'Mate'. He must have a real name, but she has no idea what it is, or any urge to find out. When she'd first moved in, she would sometimes exchange a smile or a quick word about the weather, but she soon learned not to get trapped listening to his painfully unfunny jokes, which usually take the form of rambling stories, often with a forgotten punch line. If asked, she'd probably put the beggar's age at about fifty, though it's hard to tell: he's always swathed in an assortment of oversized clothes, with a cap pulled down over his eyes. He looks too hot in summer, and too cold in winter. With no man in the house, Janine has no cast-offs to pass on to him now. Her husband died five years ago, taking with him all the laughter in their lives.

Janine's son, Calum, is on the coach of course, though in her panic his mother is unaware that she is just a few metres away from him. He's sitting next to his best friend, Rahil Nandi, who fills the fun gap with his effortless clowning. Even Miss Hunter has been known to be won over by his mischievous smile (once or twice). Now she stands up to check that all the children are still strapped in.

TICK

57 seconds to go . . .

Two girls on the coach, Charmaine and Chenelle, who sit together in class, eat together at break, and whisper together in assembly, have stopped plaiting each other's hair and are looking through the dance-class window, pointing at people they know, and half laughing, half singing '*Hey, fatty* . . .' On the other side of the aisle, a boy has spotted Bernie bending to pick up the poo. 'Gross!' he cries, making a retching noise at the back of his throat. Sitting on her own, Kayleigh Palmer, always keen to keep in with the teachers, and universally despised as a sneak, sees Lenny Gibbon outside the shoe shop, puts up her hand, and calls out Miss Hunter's name.

Lucy leans awkwardly over her eight-month bump to put the mitten back on Chloe's hand. The nearest drill falls silent, but Matey the beggar is still shouting. 'Stop a minute,' he yells, and Bernie does stay put, but only because – with creaking knees – he's struggling to find a way of grasping the dog mess without letting the hem of his fawn coat trail in the stinking residue on the pavement. He's as keen as his dog to go to the park. He wants to get the morning walk done in time to prepare the pub for the gathering after the funeral. But he wishes Ritzi would stop tugging on the lead and pulling him off balance.

The foreman of the gas workers jumps down into the trench. He's seen something he doesn't like the look of, and wants to examine it more closely. His team won't thank him if he has to stop them working to make a safety check. They want to get the job done as fast as they can, and not just so that the traffic can move smoothly again. Two of them have children at the local primary school, and if they finish early, they'll make it to the nativity play.

At the bottom of the hill, Lorraine Lee runs out of the park gates and turns towards the shops. She can feel her phone vibrating in her tracksuit pocket, but she ignores it. Can't – stop – now. Her feet are hurting, and every breath burns and stretches the inside of her chest, but Lorraine is pleased with herself. She's kept going from the moment she closed her front door, has circled the boating lake seven times, and now she's ready for the challenge of the climb towards the hot drink she's promised herself. In her mind's eye she can see the whipped cream and flakes of chocolate on top of the mug that will warm her hands as she settles into the leather sofa at the back of the café. She's conjuring up the sweet cocoa smell that in just a few minutes will be her reward. But that's not the only reason she can't afford to lose momentum. The marathon is only four months away, and she's got to build up her stamina. Who would have thought she'd get this far? When she and her friends signed up for the race it was just a joke, really, and the others dropped out long ago, defeated by the winter chill. Lorraine had never expected to get addicted to training; to long to get out of bed in the morning and into the open air. Determined to maintain the speed and rhythm of her strides, she pushes hard against the upward slope.

TOCK

56 seconds to go . . .

Eleven miles away to the east, and three thousand feet up in the air, the pilot of flight GX413 has told the cabin crew to take their seats for landing. One of the attendants is still on her feet. She's trying to persuade the passenger in seat 42A that he must take out his earphones and fold away his tray-table, but the man either can't or won't understand her, and stays still, leaning his head against the glass of the window, and staring vacantly at the clouds. He's young; probably still a teenager. The attendant knows it would be wrong to draw conclusions from the shade of his skin or his odd manner. Maybe this is his first flight and he doesn't know the rules. Perhaps he doesn't speak either of the languages in which the instructions were given. Or he might be nervous about the landing – secretly panicking, afraid to show his fear. Still, something about him is making her uneasy. She recalls that he turned down all offers of food and drink during the flight, and that on the one occasion he used the lavatory he was in there for a long time. Apologizing, she leans across the middle-aged woman on the aisle to click the man's table securely away.

On the ground, at the exit from the car park, the Audi driver, Anthony Dougall, clenches his fists as he lurches angrily towards the van that is causing the obstruction. He hears Matey shouting to Bernie: 'I've got a . . .' but takes no notice. He wants to get his car moving. Anthony is used to being in control, and until this jerk blocked the entrance to the car park with his stupid white van, he was. He had everything worked out to the split second. His wife – Gillie – thinks he's in Salzburg. He phoned her only an hour ago and peppered his conversation with little details about the weather there, the shortcomings of his hotel, the tediousness of the (non-existent) conference, and the news (gathered from the Internet) that his flight is on schedule. He assured her he would be back in good time for the family photo-shoot his agent has set up to get pictures for his election literature. Gillie thinks he's expecting a quiet birthday lunch after that, but Anthony knows (thanks to Sharon) that his wife has a 'surprise' party planned for him, with a marquee going up in the garden at this very moment. He certainly can't risk being late for that.

Bernie is prepared to tolerate Matey, since any money he collects is usually spent in the pub, and the man's not smelly, violent, or obviously mad. In fact, if the beggar's stories are to be believed, he's had quite an interesting life: time in the army; a failed attempt at stand-up comedy; then bad luck, and stupid decisions about money and women that forced him onto the streets. Still fumbling with his messy task, Bernie opens his mouth (to warn Janine, the florist, to watch where she's putting her feet) and drops the letter he was taking to the post box. It flutters down into the gas men's trench. With Lucy and the baby so close by, Bernie hopes his single swear word can't be heard above the noise of the traffic and the roadworks.

Miss Hunter is on her feet now, and as she turns, she sees that several children are standing, too. Some of them notice her, and sit down quickly.

Over to their right, the dance instructor, Maggie Tate (who, though super-fit, also likes cakes) is wearing green striped leggings under a purple leotard, and has a shocking-pink headband tied round her mass of curly hair, which is dyed an unnatural shade of red. She claps her hands and, with her back to the window, bends to switch on her old-fashioned portable cassette player. It's the size of a small suitcase, covered with unnecessary knobs and dials, and powered by a long extension lead that snakes across the floor.

'. . . *bum bum*,' sing Charmaine and Chenelle.

Kayleigh Palmer's mother is watching the exercise class, too, but with a different kind of contempt. She was in the street when the coach came by, and now, though she's got a lot to do, she doesn't want to start her errands until it's out of sight. She goes out of her way not to spoil Kayleigh, and bites her tongue if she's ever tempted to praise her or betray embarrassing signs of love, but the child is all she has since her husband left her ten years ago, and there have been times when her duty to look after Kayleigh has been her only reason for carrying on in a world so full of disappointments and unfairness. Now she's got one eye on the coach and the other on the dance studio. There's no way you'd find her in there. She thinks that extension wire is a trip hazard, for a start, but she has no intention of pointing that out to the women inside. She sniffs. People who have no qualms about cavorting about half dressed in full view of the public deserve to find out about such dangers the hard way.

'Doggie!' says little Chloe, pulling her hand away from her mother and reaching towards Ritzi's nose.

Matthew Larkin wipes his brush against the rim of the tin to get rid of any excess paint. He can't help being meticulous, even though no one else will ever see the precision with which the red line is painted. From down below, all people will get is a vague impression that the appeal fund is inching towards its target. He knows that the measurement is spot-on. He's praying (he was actually on his knees in his beloved St Michael's on Sunday) that the total will be reached in time for him to inspect the roof repairs from the top of a ladder, rather than a heavenly cloud.

TICK

55 seconds to go . . .

On flight GX413, the attendant presses the button that restores seat 41A to the upright position, ready for landing. The man still ignores her — staring through the window, clutching his MP3 player. The attendant knows it's switched on. She can hear the tinny hiss of loud music leaking from the headphones, which (against the rules) are still in his ears.

Outside the pub, where the pavement narrows opposite the church, Sarah Wilkins, aged eighty-three, is hobbling round the corner. She hasn't any specific errands to do, but the doctor has told her she needs to get out of the house every day if she wants to stay mobile, so she's on her way to the shops. Nick, the GIFTFORCE boy, seizes on her as his first challenge of the morning, stepping forward to block her path. 'A moment for the poor?' he asks, looking straight into her eyes and smiling, as he was taught on the training course. Nick had imagined that promoting good causes would make him feel good, but it's become just a job like any other: slightly worse, in fact. It's rare for shoppers to return his cheery greetings with anything other than evasiveness, and some are critical or downright rude. He used to think he liked people. Now he's not so sure.

Back down the street, Janine the florist is shifting from foot to foot, waiting to get across the road, and Matey is attempting to cheer Bernie up: '. . . joke for you.'

Janine is even more determined to get away. She doesn't want to be rude, but she hasn't time to get caught listening to one of the man's stories.

Maggie, the dance teacher, turns up the volume to compete with the din of the roadworks. With her bottom to the window as she tends the machine, she sways in time to the music, counting out the beats to get the class moving in time. 'One and . . .' Some of the women are still chatting as the others begin their routine. In the street outside, Mrs Palmer lets out a censorious sigh.

There's an alley at the side of the dance studio. It leads to the back of the funeral director's shop (or 'chapel of rest', as he would call the building, not wanting to sound too commercial). The lane opens out into a private yard. There, out of public view, the hearse is being prepared. It's an easy job today: at St Michael's, just a short drive up the road. Nevertheless, the undertaker, Frank Pilbury, is worried about timing, because the roadworks have reduced the flow of traffic to a single line, controlled by slow temporary lights. The coffin's loaded, and on a normal day the cortège wouldn't need to set off for another fifteen minutes, but today they're going to have to fight to nose their way into the solid stream of cars. There was a time when everyone would stop and make way for a funeral procession as a matter of course, but these days you can never be sure.

The undertaker's wife (a genuinely kind face for the business, but a great saleswoman too) managed to persuade the bereaved family to pay for the most expensive (or, as Frank's tasteful promotional literature puts it, 'traditional') package. It's increasingly popular, and has become a sporadic treat for the people of Heathwick since the Pilburys reintroduced it five years ago. It had long been Frank's ambition to get back to the old ways of his profession. Ever since he saw a video of *Oliver!* in the 1990s he'd dreamed of restoring the Victorian horse-drawn hearse that had long languished, dilapidated, in one of the garages at the back of the yard. When he was a child, he and his sister had used it as a den – an appropriately scary headquarters for the secret society they'd formed with their classmates from Heathwick School. In the dark, by candlelight, sitting on the spot where unnumbered corpses had rested on their final journeys, the exclusive group had played and plotted. Amidst the spiders and dust, they'd made notes, by torchlight, on the comings and goings of Mr Lorenzo, who ran (and still runs) the launderette next door. They'd been convinced (during the Falklands War of 1982) that he was an Argentinian spy.

Frank still congratulated his twelve-year-old self for taking the blame when that surveillance project got out of hand. The parents of the rest of the group knew nothing of their involvement in the writing of an anonymous note to the police. When the constable came round to see Frank's father, and Frank had been summoned into the sitting room (to discover that what, in the gloom of the hearse, Spikey Davenport had assumed to be a blank sheet of paper was in fact the reverse of a piece of headed notepaper bearing the funeral parlour's address), Frank had kept quiet about the rest of the gang. He had even written, and delivered, an embarrassing letter of apology to Mr Lorenzo. His mother had stood over him, angrily correcting his spelling and criticizing his hand-writing, as, with his tongue sticking out while he tried to concentrate, Frank laboriously scratched it out with his father's fountain pen on a sheet of the very paper that had got him into trouble. It turned out that Mr Lorenzo was Italian, not Argentinian, with an unblemished record of loyalty to his adopted home in Britain. The episode had killed off the secret society, and had not been mentioned again until the best man's speech at Charlie Morris's wedding. Charlie Morris is now a policeman in Manchester. Spikey (or rather Cyril) Davenport is a Tory MP.

In the years after the death of the secret society, the old hearse became the place where Frank experimented with smoking and drinking. Unsurprisingly, it wasn't much of a magnet for girls, and for the next twenty years or so it was almost unvisited, quietly decaying. Then, when his father (an enthusiastic modernizer) died, Frank set about the task of repairing, painting and polishing the carriage at evenings and weekends. He had carved a new filigree frieze to decorate the roof. He'd mended the spokes on the thin wheels – two huge ones at the back and two smaller at the front. He'd made a new velvet-covered plinth for the coffin, polished up the brass rails and the windows, sanded away the graffiti from the days of the den, and given the whole vehicle several coats of shiny black paint. He found an expensive decorating site online that sold silky golden tassels, and he attached one to each corner of the roof. At first, the project had been just for his own amusement, though he toyed with the idea of putting the old hearse on display in the yard.

Then, when Sidney Clark from the gang suddenly died, his widow asked if he could travel to his grave in it, and Frank had found stables where he could hire carriage-horses and a driver. After the pictures of that funeral had gone up on his website, there had been a stream of bookings for the expensive service, and Frank had grown increasingly fond of Dime and Dollar – the two jet-black stallions – who had been delivered to the yard in the early hours of this morning ready for another funeral.

So now Frank is wearing his full formal costume, a splendid outfit inherited unworn from his father (though well used by *his* father before him). It's a long frock coat, made from thick woollen fabric (that's a curse in the summer but just right for today), worn over a high-collared shirt and a black cravat. With his top hat and ebony cane, Frank can't help walking with a dignified swagger as he emerges from the alley on foot to look for a gap in the traffic and to guide the hearse forward.

On the coach, several children fail to see that Miss Hunter is on her feet. She has to shout at them, for what she suspects is the first of many times that day. The noise she makes is so familiar to the class that almost no one will take any notice. It's part gargle, part bellow, rising in volume like a vacuum cleaner that's just been switched on. 'Guuuurrrrrr 8C!' she cries.

The gas foreman has landed awkwardly on a pipe in the trench. He rubs his ankle, hoping that it's just a twist, but the electric charge of pain that shoots up his leg tells him that it's probably more serious.

Lucy, just about to stride off in the direction of her mother-in-law's house, notices that Chloe's other glove is missing, too.

TOCK

54 seconds to go . . .

The school coach lets out another acrid hiss, and inches forward before pulling up again, to an ironic cheer from the boys in the back seat.

Two large women step over Matey's feet to get to the newsagent's. The white van is in their way, and the pavement around it is crowded, with Lucy and her buggy, Bernie and his dog, the florist with her wreath, and Anthony Dougall, who has reached the white van, ready to let rip at the driver and force him to move. But the cab is empty. Anthony kicks a tyre in frustration, hurting his toe. He's got to get moving. The van blocking his path is not the first delay. After spending the night in Sharon's flat, he'd banked on an early getaway, before there were too many people about. He'd thought that choosing his birthday to tell Sharon that they'd have to cool things for a while would catch her at her most understanding, but there had been tears, and shouting, and he'd stayed in the hope of quietening her before the neighbours heard too much. Now he'll have to step on it to get out to the airport in time to buy some foreign newspapers and a present for his wife that will be at once convincingly 'foreign' (an oversized box of those chocolates they call Mozart's balls or a blingy bracelet) and yet typically 'him' (something obviously picked up in a hurry while in transit between a host of commitments more important to him than she is). He'd had everything worked out, right down to leaving the airport car park receipt (casually torn so the time won't show) lying in the foot well of the car, to bolster the deceit. And it can still work. He can still sweep into his driveway from the right direction. It's just that he left Sharon weeping in her kitchen, and he fears that if he doesn't get away soon, she might run out to catch him, and make a scene.

Matey is still talking. 'You'll like this, in . . .'

With Ritzi still pulling on the lead, Bernie is struggling to tie a knot in the top of his bag of poo, wondering whether to risk being seen dropping it into the gas men's trench, or to hang onto it until he reaches the special waste bin in the park at the bottom of the hill. Is it worth trying to retrieve the letter? It's got a cheque inside (the late payment of an overdue bill, carefully timed to arrive at the last possible moment before legal action might be set in train). He has to catch today's post with it, and he doesn't fancy going through all the rigmarole of cancelling the cheque and writing out a new one. So he stays where he is, trying to work out how to get the envelope back without straining his aching knees or losing hold of Ritzi, the boisterous puppy.

Lucy can't turn her pushchair round because the road-works have narrowed the pavement. She starts lugging it backwards towards the paper shop so she can look for the missing mitten. 'Silly old Chloe,' she says to her daughter, covering up her annoyance with a sing-song voice.

Mrs Wilkins is wearing the wrong glasses to be able to read the leaflet the charity worker is holding out to her, but he is the only person who has spoken to her today, so she stops and leans on her stick, pretending to listen, though she's left her expensive hearing aid at home, for fear of losing it in the street. Nick feels a flicker of embarrassment (almost, but not quite, a pang of shame). The chances are that the old lady can barely afford to look after herself, let alone give to others; and on another week, carrying a different clipboard, he might well find himself raising money for a charity from which she could benefit. But today it's his job to persuade her to donate, so he'll give it a try.

Over in the coffee shop, where the conversation in the queue is about education and catchment areas, Sam wishes he had the nerve to chip in with his own experiences of the school the women are discussing. He doubts whether they are picturing their beloved children wiping tables after thirteen years of lessons and homework. One little boy, unstrapped from his buggy, has escaped from his mother. He's a chubby chap, with black curly hair and a smear of chocolate around his mouth. He's wearing round, wire-rimmed spectacles, with one lens obscured to force his other 'lazy' eye to get to work. Sam knows the child's name is Max because his mother keeps breaking off from her chat to call out to him, without really taking any notice of where he is or what he's doing.

'Ma-ax!'

She's at a table Sam is not looking forward to clearing. Her little group of friends come in regularly with toddlers who are too young for school. Today they've brought glitter, scissors and cardboard, to make Christmas decorations. He's wondering whether he should ask them to leave – but he hasn't the heart. The kids seem, if anything, quieter than usual, and it is nearly Christmas. The three little girls – two of them identical, and rather beautiful twins – are bent intently over their tasks, chattering away about what Santa is going to bring them. Sam just hopes that he'll be able to get the glue off the tabletop when they eventually leave.

Max ignores his mother's call. He's pressing himself against the shop window – transfixed by a digger as it scoops out earth from the trench. Sam gets ready with his cleaning spray and his cloth. Such small hands, and yet so many smears on the glass.

Behind Max, the mourners' conversation has turned from the virtues of the deceased to reflections on the suddenness of his death. 'It makes you think . . .' says the man with the loudest voice.

In the plane, Dorothy Long – the passenger in seat 42C, two seats away from the man with the music player – rolls her eyes sympathetically at the flight attendant (who is miming the action of removing earphones, to no effect). Dorothy remembers how the young man in 42A plugged himself in early on in the flight, when she'd leaned across the empty seat between them to show off photos of the newborn grandson she's on her way to visit. She feels slightly guilty. She knows she talks too much, and fears her neighbour has frozen himself off to avoid hearing more about her life.

'. . . two and . . .' shouts Maggie, the dance instructor, getting into the rhythm of the day, and wiggling her bottom as she fiddles with the buttons on her tape player. Charmaine and Chenelle sing on, laughing. Mrs Palmer looks towards the shoe shop, and tries to catch Mrs Gibbon's eye (to invite her to share her disapproval of the shameless women behind the glass) but notices that she's got Lenny with her. Surely he should be at school? Why isn't he on the theatre trip? The expression on Mrs Palmer's face turns from indirect criticism to direct scorn. But it has no effect. Mrs Gibbon hasn't registered that she's there, and continues examining the discounted shoes.

In the funeral parlour yard behind the shops, the carriage driver (dressed, like Frank, in grand old-fashioned mourning clothes, but finishing a last cigarette before he faces the public) is holding Dime and Dollar by their bridles, ready to lead them up the alley. The horses toss their thick black manes and snort. Frank has insisted on dropping one tradition. The horses' heads are not forced back and up by painful straps, as they would have been in Victorian times. Frank is prepared to forgo a little authenticity for the sake of kindness.

TICK

53 seconds to go . . .

Maggie, the dance instructor, oblivious to the fact that she is being watched by Kayleigh's mother and the girls on the coach, jiggles on: '. . . three and . . .'

Down the hill, Lorraine Lee isn't counting. She's chanting in her head, in time to the beat of her feet against the hard paving stones. *Scan-ner*, says her inner voice. It's a trick she picked up from a running magazine. When you hit *the wall* – when the muscles in your legs are screaming that they've had enough – you can blot out their cries with an affirmation of your own. Don't let yourself think of anything but the reason why you are training. For Lorraine, it's to raise money for the cancer unit that saved, and changed, her life last year. When the doctor broke the news of her diagnosis, Lorraine had heard it as a death sentence. She'd never have imagined that the treatment, horrible though it was, would work, and leave her with a keener sense of future possibilities than she had ever felt before. Every day is precious now. For the first time ever, she has real plans – not just for the marathon, but for reunions, holidays, for making something really meaningful of her life, and for doing something for people less fortunate than herself. *Scan-ner.* It's working. Never mind the pain, she's lucky to be alive.

Her phone has stopped vibrating, too.

'Life is short,' says the loud mourner in the café, a burly man for whom this funeral is a reminder of his own mortality. The lesson he takes from it is rather different from Lorraine's. No point in going mad for fitness when death might be just round the corner anyway. Chasing the last few cake crumbs around his dentures with the tip of his tongue, he reaches into his pocket for the hip flask he put there to protect himself against the cold of the churchyard.

'Ma-ax!'

Sam wonders whether he should pull Max's messy hands off the window, but he doesn't want to frighten the child, risk the wrath of the mother, or be thought of as some kind of pervert. Through the glass, he can see the crowd gathering around the white van on the other side of the road.

There Matey is, still trying to capture Bernie's full attention: '. . . your line of work,' he says, hoping that even if his joke doesn't earn him a few coins, it might lead to a free drink later.

But Bernie's distracted by the sight of a policeman, breathless after climbing the hill, and now covering the last few metres towards them. He's pulling the radio on his lapel close to his mouth and ear to overcome the noise of the snarled traffic and the roadworks. This is PC Nigel Lewis, fresh from training school, and finding it hard to believe that anyone will ever take him seriously as an enforcer of the law. He's been dispatched from the police station to get the traffic moving again. He's got no idea how he's going to do it. It seems like no time since he would have been one of the boys on the school trip, pulling faces through the back window of the coach.

From beside the white van, Anthony Dougall, the frustrated Audi driver, calls out, 'Here! Officer!' beckoning the young constable to sort out the mysteriously empty van. Anthony is torn between doing a 'Do you know who I am?' and keeping a low profile. He doesn't want word getting back to Gillie that he's been seen in Heathwick when he's supposed to be somewhere else.

As Anthony shouts to the policeman, the school coach

makes another infinitesimal, but ear-splitting, lurch. But it still hasn't passed the dance studio. The car behind moves forward and stops suddenly, too, closing the gap through which Janine, the florist, was hoping to cross the street. She can see the plumed horses at the far end of the alley opposite, and desperately wants to get the wreath to the funeral director and into position on top of the coffin before the hearse turns into the main road. She steps back, waiting for a chance to try again, feeling it would be disrespectful to try to catch the undertaker's eye by waving.

Someone else *is* waving. This is Deanna Fletcher. She's on the other side of the road, outside the launderette. She's rushing to meet her boyfriend, Paul Broadbrook, and she's just seen him, coming in the other direction, weaving his way through the stationary traffic right up the other end of the High Street, by the church. He hasn't spotted her yet, but she would recognize that jaunty walk anywhere. His hands are in his pockets as usual, and his long multi-coloured scarf is trailing behind him as he dodges between the cars. Paul and Deanna have been apart for six weeks. He's been on a course in Scotland, and she wasn't expecting him home till tomorrow. How like him to surprise her by getting an early plane down! He phoned her half an hour ago to tell her to drop everything and meet him in the coffee shop in Heathwick. And she'd done it. She'd muttered an excuse to her boss at the call centre outside town, and before he had time to react, she'd jumped into her car and driven away. When she hit the traffic jam, she pulled into a side street and set off on foot, her heart pounding like a teenager's at the thought of seeing Paul again.

Deanna knows why he's chosen the café as their meeting place. It was where they first saw each other – when it was still the library, where she'd had a job she loved and he had come in to ask for a book she adored. Having Paul in her life was all that had got her through the shock of unemployment and then the dreariness of her new work. She'd never been impulsive. Running out of the office like that was totally out of character. But hearing Paul's voice in her headset out of the blue, she couldn't resist the drama of rushing to meet him, no matter what the consequences might be. And now he's just metres away. In a few seconds they'll be together again.

TOCK

52 seconds to go . . .

'. . . four. And . . .'

'Have you heard . . .' says Matey, apparently un-concerned by the lack of interest all around him.

Maybe Sam should speak to Max's mother, ask her to stop her son dirtying the window. But he can remember the joy of watching machinery when he was small. And anyway, the woman is busy cutting out cardboard snowflakes to keep the little girls entertained. One of them, kneeling on her chair to reach the blunt plastic scissors, has started singing: '*Trinkle, trinkle* . . .' This is Polly. Those in the know can distinguish her from her twin sister Nell because she always has a red ribbon in her curly blonde hair, while Nell's is always blue.

By the window, behind Max, the loud mourner pours

a glug of brandy into the dregs of his coffee. One of his companions looks at his watch. Another stands and turns in the direction of the loo at the back of the café.

Over the road, beyond the junction where Nick, the charity boy, has collared the old lady, the Reverend Jonathan Davis is standing in the churchyard, his cassock billowing in the wind, as he waves his arms in a half-hearted semaphore and shouts, with polite restraint, 'I say!'

He's trying to attract Matthew Larkin's attention without taking him by surprise and risking a fall from the ladder. He doesn't want to sound ungrateful to the old man, who is, he knows, only trying to help; but he wishes Matthew would get a move on. The bell has started tolling for the funeral. The coffin is due to arrive soon. Some of the early mourners have already looked askance at such a mundane activity as sign painting taking place on their special, solemn day.

But Matthew seems (and indeed may actually be) deaf to the vicar's reedy pleas. He dips his brush into the paint again, thinking about his daughter – how much he's looking forward to greeting her at the airport, and how long it's been since he's felt the squeeze of her hand, the warmth of her lips on his cheek.

Janine, the florist, takes out her mobile phone to check

the time, though she knows full well that she's more than twenty minutes late with the wreath.

'Sir! Sir!' says the flight attendant, still getting no response. She's wondering whether to report the man to the captain, but that would lead to a trail of paperwork, and this is her last shift for a week. Once they've landed, she'll want to get away as fast as she can. She's tired. Her feet, which always swell up during long-haul flights, are aching in her high-heeled shoes. Her skin has dried out after weeks of relentless exposure to the dead atmosphere of cabins, airports and plastic hotels. Her lips are cracking at the edges of her weary smile. She's longing to get into jeans, trainers and a sweat shirt and to slob around at her parents' house for a few days. Why won't this guy just do as he's told?

TICK

51 seconds to go . . .

'. . . five, and . . .'

'*Likkle shtar . . .*'

At the newsagent's, the man with the backpack, who has just asked for a nine-volt battery, has stepped away from the counter to hold the door open for the two fat ladies. The racket of the roadworks comes with them, laced with Matey's throaty roar.

'. . . the one about . . .' The beggar has raised his voice, hoping Anthony Dougall will join his audience, but he's still trying to grab the policeman's attention.

Anthony's mind is darting over alternative plans for getting on the move. There's a bus at the bottom of the hill, by the park. He knows its route ends at the airport, and it's moving so slowly that he could probably beat it to the stop halfway down the hill and have time to get on board. But his car would be left blocking the way out of the car park, and he'd only get into more trouble for that – and not just with the policeman. Gillie would be bound to hear about it.

Lenny Gibbon's mother has spotted a likely pair of shoes in a wire bin outside the shop and, as Miss Hunter expects, Lenny is dragged inside, mouthing an expletive Mrs Gibbon either misses or ignores.

In his grubby flat above the shoe shop, fifty-one-year-old Noel Gilliard, author of one well-reviewed (but largely unread) novel and several that have failed to make it into print, absent-mindedly clicks the Internet icon on his computer. Although no publisher seems interested in his work these days, he's determined to produce another book. Two days ago, he decided to implement his New Year resolution a little early (or perhaps very late indeed, since he had the same intention back in January). It's a radical change of habits, which should increase his productivity. He's promised himself that he'll get straight down to his writing first thing every morning, and will never succumb to online distractions before lunch time. Simple. Shouldn't take much willpower. And yet he's only just had breakfast, he hasn't even read through the two paragraphs he squeezed out yesterday, and he can't stop himself.

He starts typing in his Internet password: *Tolstoy*. He'll just have a little look round some of his favourite sites before getting down to some serious work.

Noel's elderly cat, Vita, is snuggled up in one of her favourite places: an old towel on the chunky radiator under the windowsill. She's nearly twenty, and sleeps almost all the time, but her honey-coloured fur is still long and lustrous, and when they are open, her eyes tell of mystery, wisdom and uncanny understanding, or so Noel believes. Since he discovered how to order cat litter and food on the net, Noel doesn't have much need to go out. Vita is the only living being he has touched for several days.

For the past half-hour, a young man in an ill-fitting suit has been sitting on a bench in the churchyard, checking and rechecking his wristwatch as it creeps towards half-past nine. He is Stuart Penton, unemployed since leaving the rather undistinguished local university more than a year ago, but now, at last, called for a job interview. He's uncomfortable. He hasn't dressed smartly since his graduation ceremony, and his relationship with the waistband of his trousers has been profoundly damaged by months of junk food and Internet gaming. He's nervous. He wants the job, even though it's only junior clerical work at the offices of the local free news-paper (which, he has been dismayed to discover, are above the run-down bakery next to the petrol station over the road). Stuart is desperate to stop living off (and with) his parents, who find it increasingly difficult to disguise their irritation at the poor return they've had on years of school fees.

This morning he had to get away from the atmosphere in the house, even though it means he's got to hang around in the cold now, because he doesn't want to look too keen by turning up early for his appointment. Over breakfast, his mother wouldn't shut up about how he must demand decent pay and conditions, and mustn't be fobbed off with unpaid work experience disguised by the label 'internship'. 'The New Slavery', she called it, in a speech he'd heard a thousand times before. His father was just as bad, warning him to be ready for tricky questions about big international news stories, quizzing him over his cereal about Arab leaders from countries he'd never heard of. Cruising the news websites and Wikipedia on his mobile phone, Stuart is using the last few minutes before his 9.30 appointment to mug up on the recent cabinet changes, and the progress of international economic deals. Nevertheless, he suspects that the editor will want to hear more about what's going on in Heathwick, and on that subject his mind (and the Internet) is blank. *Nothing ever happens here*, he thinks to himself.

But, though Stuart doesn't know it, a tiny drama is in progress across the road. A woman is hurrying out of the bakery. She's elderly, but elegant, the thinning hair beneath her felt and feather hat tinted a vibrant orangy-blonde. Her winter coat has luxurious fur cuffs, which are getting in her way as, struggling with two carrier bags, she tries to stuff her change into her purse. This is Lotte Rabane, once a star of the (long defunct) local repertory theatre, and still respected by people who can remember those days (though she's a little dotty now, and sometimes forgets her way home). She'd normally have stayed in the warmth of the baker's for a chat (and her usual joke about bloomers) but this morning she couldn't get out fast enough. It was too embarrassing: another customer was almost in tears. It didn't seem polite to stay and watch, though Lotte was intrigued by the scene, and there was a time when it would have provided her with professional material.

A thin, smart woman, probably about forty-five, was shaking like a child, obviously in the early stages of a panic attack, as a magnificent cake, lusciously decorated with shards of dark chocolate and glistening cherries, was being eased into a gigantic box. The baker was trying to persuade Gillie Dougall (for whom today is the culmination of months of planning for her husband's surprise birthday party) that the cake will easily feed seventy guests. He's right, but Gillie is picturing the scene if it's finished before everyone has been served. In her mind, the possibility has now become an inevitability – the worst catastrophe of her life. This is what Gillie does. She panics. When her anxiety engine is firing, there is nothing she can do to stop it, and today it's going to be powering a waterwheel of worry. She's in no doubt now. She's ordered an inadequate cake, and so Anthony's party is going to be a disaster. His political career will be irrevocably damaged. And it's all her fault.

Lotte Rabane has recognized Gillie. She knows she idolizes her husband. But she also knows, because she lives next door to a young woman called Sharon Carter, that Gillie's faith in him is misplaced. There was nothing for it: Lotte had to leave the shop before she said something she might regret.

TOCK

50 seconds to go . . .

'. . . six, and . . .' Maggie Tate is getting into her stride.

Matey continues his joke: '. . . two old friends called . . .'

'. . . *how wa wardur* . . .' sings Polly, rubbing a handful of glitter onto her face.
  'Ma-ax!'

Through the wall next to his desk, Noel Gilliard can hear Mariam, a recent arrival from the Middle East who rents a cheap room over the dance studio. She is running a bath. As ever, the hot water is coming out in noisy air-locked burps from the old-fashioned boiler in the shared bathroom. Noel blames her burst of activity for killing his creativity this morning. That, and the racket from the roadworks outside. Cursing the drills, he clicks again – this time on the link to a chat site where authors complain to each other about publishers, agents and booksellers, while lavishing insincere flattery on each other's work.

Downhill from the funeral parlour alley, in the launderette opposite the newsagent's, Marco Lorenzo is oblivious to the upheaval in the street outside. There is a problem with his dry-cleaning machine, an old self-service model, installed by one of his predecessors in the 1970s. It's hard to get spare parts for it now, and the volatile fluid on which it depends has been leaking through an ancient valve. Marco has been trying to fix it for over an hour, and the fumes are giving him a headache. He calls to his son, Stefano, hoping he'll lend a hand, but Stefano has just left, to buy some cigarettes at the newsagent's over the road.

On the coach, Calum and Rahil duck down so that Miss Hunter can't see them. The headmaster has banned all mobiles and music players, but Rahil has smuggled his big sister's smartphone on board, and the two boys are sharing the headphones – one ear each. They're laughing at her dubious taste in Bollywood musicals and looking up rude things on the Internet at the same time. Calum's hoping Rahil will ask him back to his house after the trip. He loves it there. Not just because of the garden, the pets, and the seemingly constant supply of home-cooked food, but because of the size of the family – still intact, unlike his own – and replete with brothers and uncles for football, cricket, and fun. They even have a basketball net in the garden – a garden! And the biggest television set in town. The Nandis' home is a wonderful refuge from his own – with his batty granny and his harassed mother, and the over-powering embarrassment of living a life funded (extremely inadequately) by selling flowers.

Outside the bakery, Lotte Rabane, flustered, and hampered by her cream leather gloves, drops the money she is trying to put in her purse. Coins roll in all directions across the pavement.

Nearby, at the service station, a petrol tanker is beginning a routine delivery. The driver was held up in the traffic on his way here, and he's running behind schedule. He attached the pipe as quickly as he could. Now, as the counter races round, clocking up how much fuel has been pumped into the underground tanks, his eyes are on Matthew Larkin painting his sign in the churchyard. He hasn't seen the tiny hole in the tube, or the growing puddle of petrol on the forecourt.

. TICK

49 seconds to go . . .

In the café, Polly, the little girl with the glittery cheek, continues her incomprehensible carol: '. . . *washu ar.*' Max's mother exchanges a loving smile with the twins' mum across the table.

Paul Broadbrook, reaching the kerb after finding a pathway through the traffic, stoops to pick up the coins for Lotte, whom he's seen around Heathwick many times over the years. Though the two have nodded the occasional greeting, they've never spoken. From the other end of the street, his girlfriend, Deanna Fletcher, sees his head bob out of view, and wonders what has happened.

Matey bashes on: '. . . Jack and Pete who . . .'
Bernie is amused to see Anthony Dougall getting ever

more agitated and the florist shuffling from foot to foot, struggling to communicate with the funeral director without looking frivolous. Bernie's resigned to staying put until he has thought of a way to get his envelope out of the trench. Ritzi, however, still has other ideas. Her mind is on the park. The lead is growing tighter. She barks.

Across the street, Lenny Gibbon is trying to pull his mother out of the shoe shop. He wishes he was on the coach with his classmates, even though he spent hours last night moaning about the stupid theatre trip. He's seen the coach stuck in the road, and is wondering whether Miss Hunter would let him get on. She'd be angry, of course. She'd want an explanation for why he didn't turn up in the first place, but he could blame his mother for keeping him off school, even though the reality was that he'd refused to go. Anything would be better than this shopping.

Upstairs from the Gibbons, Noel Gilliard has entered another password (*Proust*), and is clicking again. He's thinking of starting a new discussion thread about sources of inspiration, even though he's rather short of them at the moment.

Through the wall, Mariam unzips her wash bag to look

for a tiny bottle of shampoo she picked up when cleaning a hotel bathroom. It's one of the few perks of her job as a chambermaid, though most of the customers, especially the rich ones, take all the free toiletries home with them when they leave. She's only allowed to keep containers that have already been opened, but there's often enough in them for a hair wash or bubble bath, and they can be mixed together to make more. This morning Mariam plans a long soak. Last week she swapped shifts with a friend who was after a free weekend, and this is her first break for ages. She'd never have imagined, back in her homeland a year ago, that she would leave her laboratory and find herself living alone, and cleaning toilets, so far away. But who could have known that politics could move so fast, and that her family would become targets of the new regime in her country? Her bedsit might be dreary, and her work long and hard, but at least she feels safe here. And not just that. Today there is some hope. She's got an appointment with someone who might have news about her family. There's a chance she'll find out at last whether her father and brother are dead or alive.

In front of the school coach, a taxi driver is drumming his fingers on the steering wheel, as upset as anyone by the hold-up, even though his meter is still running. There's a bank to his left, and his passenger has asked him to unlock the door so he can get out to use the cash machine. The temporary traffic lights controlling the contraflow are pointless now. His line of traffic was let through just as the digger got in the way, and now the lights behind them are changing ineffectively: red – green – red – while he, the coach, and a handful of cars block the only lane. With the digger still manoeuvring slowly in the middle of the road, and at least three cars in front of him, the taxi driver is pretty sure he won't have a chance to move far before the man gets back. The passenger – who speaks little intelligible English – seems rather jumpy, but that's not surprising, since he's stuck in a traffic jam on his way to the airport. With all the time it takes to get through airport security these days, the poor bloke must be worrying about being late.

Kayleigh has noticed her mother, though Mrs Palmer is still looking into the dance studio.

'. . . STRETCH, seven . . .'

Kayleigh taps on the window of the coach and shouts, 'Mummy!'

Her mother grimaces as, for what seems like the hundredth time that morning, a mechanical voice comes from the digger: '*Attention, this vehicle . . .*'

TOCK

48 seconds to go . . .

'*. . . is reversing!*'

The boys in the seats around Kayleigh imitate her prissy voice, making it sound more stuck up and plummy than it actually is: 'Mummeh! Euh, Mummeh!'

The taxi driver releases the lock on the back door of his cab, confident that his passenger will get to the cash machine and back before the cab has moved more than a few metres.

Bernie has noticed the gas foreman down in the trench, just a few metres from where he is standing. He calls out to him, speaking over the next line of Matey's joke ('. . . ran into each other . . .'), in the hope of persuading the workman to come along and pick up his envelope.

But the man is preoccupied. Though clearly in pain from his twisted ankle, he is closely examining one of the pipes.

Constable Lewis steps gingerly between Ritzi and the edge of the roadworks, trying to work out why Anthony Dougall is shouting and pointing at the white van. Behind Anthony's own car, which is stuck in the exit from the car park with its front door wide open, a line of vehicles has built up. They are honking their horns.

Janine, the florist, has at last caught the funeral director's eye. He signals to her, with a wave of his ebony cane, that he will find a way across to collect the wreath. It's too late to incorporate it in the display of flowers on top of the coffin. He's already decided to carry it himself, as he walks ahead of the cortège, in traditional style.

Back down the alley, the carriage driver stubs out his cigarette and rummages in his pocket for a paper bag full of sugar cubes for Dime and Dollar. The two horses read his mind, and nuzzle his neck. He pats them tenderly. He wants to keep them calm. The turn into the main road and those first few metres along the narrow stretch of tarmac by the roadworks are going to be a challenge for the beasts. He hopes the undertaker will be able to negotiate with the gas men to stop their drilling long enough for the hearse to get past.

'. . . and eight.' Maggie's voice is full of joy. It's not just a way of encouraging her less enthusiastic clients. She really *is* happy today. When her classes are over she's going to collect the tickets for her holiday: ten days in Thailand while the dance studio is closed over Christmas. It's her first reward for the hard work she's put into building up her fitness business.

Up near the junction, a couple of doors down from the pub, alongside the noisy digger and opposite the bakery, Doreen Talbot is locking her door, even though her wedding-dress shop (Doreen's Dreams) has been open for less than half an hour. She's angry with herself and with the world. Yesterday, she popped across to the shoe-shop sale just for a moment, and the mail came when she was out. The postman couldn't leave an important package without getting a signature. Now she will have to go to the sorting office to collect it. She can't be bothered to rewrite her BACK IN 5 MINUTES sign, even though she knows she's bound to be away for longer.

Doreen's upstairs tenant, Terry Potts, an art teacher at the adult education college in a nearby town, is at his window, craning his neck to see what is going on below him. Terry has been on the phone off and on since the small hours, trying to pull his oldest friend out of a trough of despair that's verging on the suicidal. He's a good listener, but he's tired, and he's running late. His friend was slow to open up, but now his flow can't be stopped, and Terry is letting him ramble on about his problems, in the hope that talking will make him feel better.

Looking down, Terry recognizes Doreen's back-combed hair bobbing about as she turns the key in the lock, and notices that she's thinning a bit on top. To think that he quite fancied her when he first moved in! Now he's more interested in the florist next door. She doesn't seem to have a man in her life. But he's keeping his distance. He's learned a lot about her through the wall that divides their two flats. Her overweight son can be a bit of a pain, and her mother shrieks and howls at all hours, trapped in some unknown misery from long ago. Terry should be on his way to work. If the phone hadn't rung he would have had a good night's sleep and be well away from Heathwick by now, but he knows it's more important to help his friend – even though today there's a meeting with the management about cuts at the college, and turning up late won't help his case for staying on.

Across the road, Paul Broadbrook, trying to help collect

Lotte Rabane's dropped coins, steps on the end of his own long scarf, and topples to the ground.

In the café, Polly's twin sister, Nell, and her little friend, Lily, have joined in the song. '*Wow I wugner . . .*'

'Beats this rubbish,' says the girl behind the counter, laughing as she turns down the canned Christmas music that she's been forced to play since October.

TICK

47 seconds to go . . .

Miss Hunter flicks her hair behind her ears and lets loose another doomed disciplinary call: 'Guuuurrrrrr 8C!'

Outside the launderette, Deanna is wondering what's happened to Paul. Did she really see him in the distance, or is her mind playing tricks on her? She crosses the undertaker's alley towards the dance studio.

'REACH! One . . .'

The undertaker steps off the kerb, holding up his cane to stop the traffic, even though there is little prospect of it moving.

Mariam, looking down from her bathroom window

above the dance studio, smiles at his extravagant gesture. She recognizes the song booming from the dance class downstairs and joins in, further annoying Noel next door. He is reading a message from a fellow author who, Noel thinks, is trying to make his colleagues feel small by complaining about the burden of having to answer fan mail.

The taxi passenger gets out.

Terry Potts makes sympathetic noises as his friend continues his tale of woe. He can't hear everything that's said because of the noise of the diggers and drills and the tolling funeral bell. As he listens, he catches sight of an odd-looking girl. Her face is almost completely obscured by a balaclava. She's wearing thick tights and sensible shoes, with the strap of a bulky canvas bag slung diagonally across a hooded jacket that's ridiculously large. It looks almost as if she has been padded out to disguise her real shape, like a slim actress playing a fat woman in a play. She is taping a sign to the lamppost outside the pet shop next door, before the bank. Because of the angle, Potts has to press himself right up against the window to see what she is doing. He doesn't know it, but he is an ageing mirror-image of three-year-old Max across the road in the café. The butter left on Terry's hands by the toast he rustled up with the phone pressed into his shoulder even makes similar finger marks on the glass.

'Ma-ax!'

Stuart Penton feels awkward sitting in the churchyard now that people have started arriving for a funeral. He stands, and locks the buttons on his mobile phone. It looks as if it might rain, but the pub isn't open yet, so he can't go in there. Perhaps he'll head down to the newsagent's to buy a bar of chocolate before his interview.

On flight GX413, the attendant reaches over again and gently pulls the headphones from the passenger's ears. 'Turn it off,' she says. He still won't meet her eyes.

'. . . quite by chance?' says Matey, reaching the end of the set-up for his joke.
    Bernie isn't really listening, but he's got the idea that it's going to be a tale of two old friends. He calls out to the gas man again, gesticulating at the envelope lying in the mud at the bottom of the trench.

'Doggie! Doggie!' cries young Chloe, as Lucy pulls her pushchair away towards the newsagent's shop.

Doreen spots the postman with his little cart making his

way down the other side of the street. How ridiculous that she has to walk all the way to the sorting office when he was coming back today anyway! But she knows there's no choice. The red-and-white card the postman left yesterday makes it clear that she must collect the package in person, and take ID with her.

The parcel is likely to be a veil specially ordered for a wedding tomorrow. In fact, Doreen is depending on it being that, and not some stupid sample from a supplier. The bride's dress has been altered to fit her ever-shrink-ing form, and is hanging at the back of the shop, ready to be delivered this evening. If the head-dress is missing, there is likely to be another volcano of tears like the one on Thursday at the final fitting. And it won't just spoil a young girl's special day, it will cost Doreen dearly. Used to pre-wedding nerves, she comforted the panicking girl (and her mother) when she lost faith in her previous choice, an elaborate confection of feathers and flowers. She reassured the bride that there would be no problem ordering a replacement, and promised her mother a refund if it failed to arrive in time. Doreen has no intention of telling them that it proved far more difficult than she expected to get hold of the diamanté-and-lace tiara, or that she had paid extra for swift delivery because she genuinely couldn't bear the idea of a bride walking down the aisle with disappointment in her heart. What a dunce she had been to be out yesterday.

And now, who knows what she will miss by going off to the sorting office? There might be a new customer on her way, full of hope and clutching a credit card, destined only to find a locked door. Doreen wishes she could stay in her shop, and wants to get the unwelcome trip over as soon as possible.

TOCK

46 seconds to go . . .

The boys on the coach take no notice of Miss Hunter's call, and some even mimic her hair-flick as they repeat the cry of 'Mummeh!'

Charmaine and Chenelle are on another round of '*Fatty bum, bum,*' and Calum and Rahil, though successfully hiding from view, are clearly up to no good. There are two give-away signs: they are laughing extremely loudly, and they have not joined in the mass teasing of Kayleigh Palmer.

At St Michael's, Ben Whatmore, long a thorn in the vicar's side, has stopped by the thermometer sign. Reverend Davis knows what to expect: a lecture about the folly of raising money to repair the roof, and how the Church's human mission (saving souls and mending tattered lives) is more important than tending old buildings. The vicar hasn't got time to engage in the argument, which is just as well, since he might not put the opposite case too well. Though fond of St Michael's ancient stones, he has a lot of sympathy for Ben's view. But he's near retirement, and hasn't enough energy to take on the enthusiastic group of locals who value the building as much as (or even more than) its purpose. And right now, drizzling with a cold, and facing a busy day, he's more interested in getting Matthew and his ladder safely out of the way before the funeral.

Behind him, Stuart Penton notices that one of his shoelaces has come undone. He bends down to tie it up.

Across the road from them, Paul is reassuring Lotte that he is unharmed, though he's bleeding profusely from a small cut near his eyebrow. Still on the ground, he's picking up some of the lost coins.

Looking down at the street, Terry Potts, the art teacher, has missed Paul's tumble. He's concentrating on the girl sticking up the poster outside the pet shop. She's Kate Daintree. She's seventeen and, like Sam, Deanna, Anthony Dougall and Terry himself, she should really be somewhere else. Her parents think she's at her expensive private school. She left the house in full uniform as usual, and she's still wearing it under the huge cagoule that makes her look comically overweight though she's actually quite petite. She's borrowed the coat and balaclava from Jon, her first real boyfriend, who has changed her life and possibly determined her destiny.

Terry is assuming that her sign is an appeal for help to find a lost cat or dog. He's wrong. Doreen is the first to take a close look, as she tucks her keys into her handbag. Kate is fastening down the last bit of tape, and over her shoulder Doreen can see that the poster is an attack on the pet shop for selling captive animals.

Matey continues his joke, even though he's not sure whether anyone is paying attention: 'Jack was absolutely . . .'

Across the road, Maggie Tate reaches higher: '. . . and two . . .'

Charmaine and Chenelle copy the move, slamming their hands against the luggage rack above their heads. Rory Lennahan is opening up his packed lunch. Kayleigh Palmer sees him doing it and shouts, 'Miss!'

The funeral director is slimmer than the florist, and, wrapping his precious coat tightly around himself to make sure it doesn't catch on the exhaust pipe, he manages to shuffle sideways between the back of the coach and the Mini following it, which helpfully reverses a few crucial inches without bumping into the car behind. The driver, Sally Thorpe, is recalling advice her granddad gave her years ago, when she was first learning to drive: *Never get behind something you can't see through.* He was right. With no idea what is up ahead, she can't tell how long she is likely to be stuck here. She's pretty sure she's going to be late for work. Yet she's half hoping that the traffic flow will still be slow a little further along, when she's passing Doreen's Dreams, just in case there's a special dress in the window. It's not that Gavin has actually asked her to marry him, but she has high hopes. It's a long time since she's been so happy. She's longing for tonight, when they're meeting for dinner at an Italian restaurant near his office.

A little up ahead to her right, just as joyful, but now a little anxious, Deanna is craning her neck for another sight of Paul. Maybe it wasn't him in the distance after all.

The driver of the public bus, a hundred metres down the hill, has lost hope of reaching the next stop soon. He gives in to appeals from his passengers and, defying the rules, presses the button to open the door early, so they can get out and walk. Some are wearing black. Even though they thought they had left plenty of time for the bus ride to the funeral, it seems that their best bet for getting to the church on time is to go on foot.

In the launderette, Marco has managed to loosen the faulty valve. He needs to clean it, but it mustn't be detached for too long. Without the bung in place, the fumes from the belly of the machine are overpowering.

TICK

45 seconds to go . . .

Although Doreen has never liked Mr Eglington, who runs the pet shop, she doesn't approve of the girl sticking up her sign. But she can't leave her own premises shut for long, so there's no time to stop and argue. She turns, to hurry on – away from the shops and the roadworks, and round the corner past the pub in the direction of the sorting office. It's a long uphill walk.

She'll pass the churchyard, where Stuart Penton hears the unmistakable sound of his trousers ripping as he bends to tie his shoelace.

As Mariam sings on, Noel Gilliard opens a new page to compose a tart message for the authors' chat room about the agony of living next door to a tone-deaf foreigner. What's the woman doing in this country anyway? He's never actually spoken to her, but he's seen her coming and going. Her luscious black curls and swarthy skin leave him in little doubt that she's from the Middle East, though her western clothes suggest that she is probably not a religious extremist. He assumes that she's come to take advantage of the benefits system. For all he knows, she's here illegally. She may have plans to fill her room with relatives and friends. Maybe he'll write to the council about her. If he can find the time.

'... and three ...' Maggie's looking at a turquoise T-shirt one of her fitter clients is wearing, and thinking that she'd like to get one the same shade for her holiday.

The taxi driver watches his passenger walk towards the cash machine. One of the mourners from the coffee shop is dodging across the road through the traffic jam and looks as if he is making for the bank too. Who will get there first? Will the taxi passenger have to wait? The driver looks ahead for somewhere to pull in should the traffic start moving too soon.

As Lucy tugs her pushchair backwards towards the newsagent's, her unborn baby reminds her of its presence with the thump of its foot. Even though this happens several times a day (and even more often at night), it still feels odd to her to have part of her body absolutely out of her control – like a muscle moving of its own accord. Instinctively, her hand comes off the buggy to rub her tummy – not so much to comfort herself, as to say hello to the little one she already knows so well but will be meeting for the first time very soon.

'. . . thrilled to see . . .'

Only half listening to Matey, Bernie looks up the street towards the church, and spots Nick the fundraiser talking to old Mrs Wilkins. Bernie notices her stick, with its curved handle. He can't yet see the cyclist who is freewheeling downhill past the pub. Anticipating the temporary traffic controls, he's riding on the pavement, unaware that Nick and the old lady are in his path just round the bend.

The door of the launderette opens. Someone has arrived with a large bag of dirty clothes, wanting to drop them off for a service wash. Marco is still on his hands and knees at the base of the dry-cleaning machine.

The flight attendant is losing patience. Although she's never actually heard of an MP3 player bringing down a plane, rules are rules, and it's her job to get the machine switched off while the plane is approaching the airport. The man can't be listening to it any more, anyway, now that she's removed his headphones. But his grip on the machine tightens as she tries to take it away.

TOCK

44 seconds to go . . .

Way down the hill, on the steep incline from the park, Lorraine Lee is breathing hard, but still determined to keep going. *Scan-ner.*

'. . . and four.' Maggie would like a new bikini as well, but she's not sure where she'd find one in Heathwick at this time of year.

Frank, the funeral director, who has now arrived on the newsagent's side of the street, gathers that the beggar is telling one of his jokes and, as the florist starts to gush apologies for being so late with the wreath, he tunes in to Matey's story.
  '. . . his old friend.'

Bernie is tuning out. He's formulating a new plan for

retrieving the letter. He'll borrow the old lady's walking stick and try to fish the envelope out of the trench himself. He'd go up to Mrs Wilkins, and rescue her from the annoying young man, but Ritzi is still pulling in the opposite direction, and staying still is hard enough. He hates to think how Ritzi would react if he started walking away from the park, so he stays put in the hope that the old woman will come to him.

The cyclist, flying round the corner, pulls on his brakes as he finds Nick and Mrs Wilkins in his way.

In the shoe shop, Mrs Gibbon is asking the assistant to measure Lenny's feet. What does she think he is, some sort of child? He makes a lurch for the door, but his mother grabs his wrist as if he were a four-year-old. His hatred for her is reaching new heights.

Like Lenny, Mrs Gibbon is wishing he had gone on the theatre trip after all. She's regretting being so weak this morning when he refused to leave for school. She's determined, now, to establish some authority. He needs new shoes, and she's going to make sure he gets them. That way the day won't be completely wasted. And since she's paying, they'll get the shoes she chooses. It's as simple as that. The boy needs to learn some respect. She's not going to give in this time. Lenny needs discipline, and it's her job to provide it. He won't thank her in the long run if she caves in every time he protests. How did she get in this mess? How did her cheerful, cheeky little child turn into this nasty teenager? Is that her fault too?

Unaware of the flood of bile lapping against the other side of the wall, Mariam is trying to attach a perished rubber shower hose to the bath taps. She hasn't bothered to turn the taps off, and accidentally squirts water all over her pyjamas.

Someone has stopped alongside Kayleigh Palmer's mother by the plate-glass window of the dance studio. He raises his mobile phone to take a photo. Maggie, the dance instructor, doesn't know it, but her landlord has sold the site, and this man is an architect who has been hired to plan the renovations. One of the exercisers sees him looking in, draws the wrong conclusion about the motive for the photograph, and sticks out her tongue.

If she'd known who employed him, she might have done worse. He's working for a big supermarket chain which has been trying for ages to get a foothold in Heathwick – one of the few local shopping streets where most of the businesses are still in private hands. They're planning a miniature version of their big brand, although they must know that shoppers come to Heathwick from all over the area simply because its

High Street still looks different from all the others. But things have already started to change. Despite the fuss over the coffee shop before it opened, many people who signed the petition against it have been unable to resist its lure. Belinda Davis, the vicar's middle-aged daughter, who is secretary of the 'Keep Heathwick Special' campaign, is tucking into a chocolate muffin at this moment.

Deanna Fletcher, just a few metres from the coffee shop now, stands still to let the man take his photographs. She can't wait to meet Paul, but she's too polite to ruin the shot, and too shy to want to be in the picture.

'Blimey!' coughs the man who has just walked into the launderette with a bin bag full of washing, only to be met by the fumes from the dry-cleaning fluid. Without looking up, Marco calls out for Stefano, hoping he'll see to the customer – but Stefano is still across the road, queuing for his cigarettes, and chiding himself for his automatic suspicion of the new arrival at the shop: a bearded man with a large backpack, who's selecting a battery from the stand by the counter. Stefano of all people, swarthy, and sometimes bearded himself, should know that appearances can mislead. He's been stopped by the police, apparently on no evidence other than his looks, more than once. And what if the battery the man has chosen is one of those little oblong things that the London bus bomber used to set off his device? Maybe the man needs it for a smoke alarm. *Crazy. Get a grip. No reason to interfere.*

On the coach, Rory Lennahan is leaning across the aisle, pointing a cold sausage at Kayleigh Palmer. 'Miss!' Miss Hunter, fiddling with her hair again, is trying to make out what is happening on the road ahead. Through the windscreen she can see the taxi in front of them, and some small cars ahead of that, then the digger in the middle of the road. The digger is the only vehicle that's moving, and it's going sideways, blocking the full width of the street. She looks at her watch and sighs.

At the front of the line of cars coming the other way, Barbara Lapsom has a clear view up the side road between the church and the pub. She knows it's no use turning into it: the street snakes round and would end up taking her back where she's come from. She saw the bike coming down the pavement, and could tell that it might hit the old lady, but there was nothing she could do about that. There wasn't even time to sound her horn – and anyway, what use would that have been with so many others going off, uselessly, all around her as delayed drivers try to vent their frustration? In a swift reflex, Barbara puts her hands over her eyes, hoping for a near-miss. She's angered by the cyclist ignoring the rules, but she's even more furious with herself for obeying her satnav's instructions. She'd heard about the emergency gasworks in Heathwick, but hadn't realized that the machine would take her straight through them on its robot route.

In her sixties herself, Barbara is on her way to the old people's home where her elderly father has just moved in. He's increasingly frail, and she is the only family he has. She'd promised herself she would never put him in an institution, but she can no longer lift him, and he needs professional care. He's been brave about selling his own house, but when she left him in his new room last night, his face crumpled in despair. She knows he will worry if she is late for her first visit, and the thought of his childlike panic is making her anxious too. The lights in front of her have automatically turned green several times, but with the digger filling the road ahead she hasn't thought it safe to move forward. The cars coming the other way are blocking the single lane available to both streams of traffic, and she's leaving them a way out for when the digger moves away, to avoid making the gridlock worse. So far, she's ignored the angry tooting of the drivers behind her, but maybe next time the green light comes, she'll give in to their urging and move forward anyway, hoping for the best.

The digger's reversing alarm starts up again. In the café, little Max joins in with the '*Beep, beep.*'

As two customers dive for a table that's becoming vacant, Sam clears it for them, picking up half-empty mugs and discarded chunks of carrot cake. The total value of the undrunk coffee and uneaten food left by just these two customers is probably about the same as half an hour's pay for him. No wonder the coffee chain is doing so well.

There's no time for Stuart to get home to change his trousers. He can feel the cold wind through the split in the seam. He wishes he hadn't worn his lucky Mickey Mouse pants today. They must show through the gap. He sees the bike on its doomed course towards Mrs Wilkins, and he doesn't want to get involved.

The flight attendant can see the shape of a mobile phone in the recalcitrant passenger's top pocket. She guesses that it is switched on, too.

TICK

43 seconds to go . . .

'STRETCH! Five . . .' With her back to the window, Maggie knows nothing about the photographer.

Stuart tries to pull down his jacket to cover the split in his trousers. There's no hope. It's too short.

In his flat above Doreen's Dreams, Terry Potts, the art teacher, is still listening to his friend, but he's also wondering what it's like to be a digger driver, and whether he'd have the nerve to hold everybody up like that. As he contemplates redundancy, he's not sure what he envies most: that the man gets to drive a digger, or that he has a job at all.

The mourner reaches the cash machine before the taxi

passenger, and the taxi driver decides that in case the man is not back before the traffic starts to move, he will risk mounting the pavement for a few metres, dodging round the digger, and pulling in to the petrol station on his right to wait. He might even get some diesel while he's there. Before embarking on his daring manoeuvre, he presses the button to wind down the nearside window and leans across, ready to shout to his passenger to explain.

In the coffee shop, Max is trying to say, '*Attention, this vehicle . . .*'

Juliet Morgan has reached the front of the queue. She's been waiting ages, because of the time it takes the school-run mothers to choose for themselves, consult those toddlers who can talk, find their purses in their giant bags of nappies and toys, and steer their massive chariots away from the counter. Juliet has been watching them, biting her tongue to stop herself telling them to sign up for the diet plan that has so transformed her own size. She's back on real food now, after months of living like an astronaut on packaged powders, but she knows she must still be careful. She's experienced an exquisite mixture of envy and contempt as one woman after another has been handed doughnuts, pastries, croissants and scones. Now it's her turn. 'Just a black coffee,' she says, with proud determination. Juliet would normally steer clear of the temptations offered by the coffee shop, but she's had to nip in today. The café has free WiFi and, held up on her way to work, she needs to get onto the Internet quickly. She wants to bid on a designer evening dress that's coming up on an auction site. It's exactly the right size for her new body, and in the photograph it looks like a perfect match for the colour of her favourite shoes. The dress would normally be way outside her price range, but unless there are lots of last-minute bidders, it will be a real bargain. It would be perfect for the Christmas cruise she's booked as a reward for all her efforts. She wants to spend the festivities with people who never knew her old, fat self. She wants to make new friends – perhaps even one special friend.

The auction is due to end at 09.22.20. Juliet has already switched on her laptop and logged on to the site. The red countdown timer is showing just over a minute to go. She knows from experience that it would be a mistake to put her bid in now: it will only force others to counter-bid and push up the price. She needs to slam in her maximum offer when they no longer have time to respond. She'll press the button just seconds before the time runs out. So now she's balancing her computer in her arms as she waits to be served, glancing at the screen from time to time, ready to click 'return' twenty seconds before the end of the auction, at 09.22.00.

Upstairs, Mariam screams, recoils from the jet of water and gropes for a towel.

Through the wall, Noel Gilliard curses her for stopping her song just when he wanted to write about it.

At the mouth of the car park, Anthony Dougall is pointing at the white van and shouting. The policeman reaches for his radio. Bernie assumes he is asking someone to find the name of the owner of the van – though it's hard to imagine what good that will do. Even if it turns out to be someone they all know, how will they find him? Where will he move the van?

Bernie misses the next line of the joke. The beggar puts on the first of the two voices he'll use to tell the tale. This is Jack, cast by Matey as a hefty cockney: 'He said, "It's great . . ."'

TOCK

42 seconds to go . . .

' ". . . to see you, but . . ." ' The beggar is still setting the scene, and despite all the distractions, Bernie and Frank the undertaker have both got the picture: in the world of the joke, two old friends have run into each other unexpectedly.

Stuart decides that buying a bar of chocolate is probably not a good idea. His trousers have told him that he's had a few too many already, and he doesn't want to display his lucky pants to the shoppers in the street. He turns to make his way up the hill, to kill the last few minutes before his appointment.

The cyclist spits out a swear word as the bike comes to a halt, its front wheel less than an inch from Mrs Wilkins. Nick, the charity worker, finds himself automatically saying 'Sorry,' even though he knows he's not in the wrong.

Across the road, outside the bakery, Paul starts getting up from the pavement, his hand full of coins. Lotte puts down her carrier bags and tries to help him to his feet.

On the coach, Rory Lennahan uses his teeth to break into a packet of salt-and-vinegar crisps. Beside him, Josh Johnson rummages on the floor and pulls a six-pack of fizzy drinks from his bag. Kayleigh is still shouting 'Miss!' but Miss Hunter is concentrating on the shoe shop now, half hoping the coach won't have moved on when Lenny Gibbon and his mother come out. She would hate to miss the chance to glare at them – to let them know that she's seen what they're up to.

Some of the mourners leave the coffee shop.
   '*Ith wiverthin,*' lisps Max.

'Anything with it?' the girl behind the counter asks Juliet Morgan, not realizing the cruelty of the question.

'. . . and six . . .'

Up at the church, the vicar, who knows he has neither the time to indulge in, nor any hope of winning, an argument with Ben Whatmore about ecclesiastical priorities, has also given up trying to get the painter and his ladder out of the way in time for the funeral. He turns back towards the church, ready to walk over and greet the mourners. He's struggling to get into the right frame of mind to conduct the service. He knows that neither the dead man nor his family were believers, and doubts whether the finer points of the ritual will mean much to anyone. There was a time when he might have seen the event as a chance to change minds or win hearts, but today he can't help hoping that this will be one of the last funerals he has to do before the blessed day of his retirement, only six months away now. As the bell tolls on, and the first notes of organ music drift over from the church, Reverend Davis cringes at the thought of the mawkish music the family have chosen: *We Are Sailing*, the theme tune from a TV drama, and the inevitable *My Way*. He guesses that few of the congregation will know the words to the only hymn. But he knows they will be reviewing his performance as if he were an actor in a play.

The taxi driver yells across the street to his passenger, hoping to explain that he'll pick him up at the petrol station, but it seems he can't be heard over the din. The man does not respond.

The gas foreman in the trench is also shouting, trying to tell his workmates something, but he can't be heard either.

'Show me your phone,' says the flight attendant firmly. The man still stares straight ahead. He mutters something in a guttural accent.

Marco balances the valve on the bench by the dry-cleaning machine and stands up to deal with his customer.

TICK

41 seconds to go . . .

'. . . and seven . . .'

'Good morning,' says Marco, wiping his hands on his trousers. The valve rolls off the bench and onto the floor. The fumes are still escaping from the open pipe.

Over the road, Matey's whole body is transformed as he gets himself into character as cockney Jack: ' "Why so sad?" '

Frank, the funeral director, looks across at the alley. Dime and Dollar seem settled, and for now there is no prospect of being able to lead them out into the road. He can stay to hear more of the beggar's tale.

Bernie notices the look of concern on the face of the

workman in the trench. Is he grimacing about the pain in his ankle, or is he worried about something else?

Outside the baker's shop, Paul steps on the end of his scarf once more, and falls back down. Gillie Dougall is now carrying a large white box, and as she leaves the bakery, she almost stumbles over him. Gillie has accepted that she'll have to live with the cake. There's no time to get a bigger one now. She's even feeling a little concerned about letting her anxiety show, and worries that she might have offended the baker, who has done such a good job, matching her specifications exactly. No, if anyone is to blame, it's herself, as usual. She'll just have to work harder to make everything else at the lunch exactly right: the balloons, the flowers, the canapés and the string quartet. But first she must get the cake safely into her car, for which she found a parking spot just before the way in and out of the car park was blocked by the white van. Peering over the top of the box, she's looking for a way across to the other side of the road. She hasn't spotted her husband shouting at the policeman, and he has not seen her.

Standing at the counter in the coffee shop, Juliet Morgan eyes up the cakes and biscuits, mentally tasting the sweet, damp, warm puffiness of the *pain aux raisins*, even though she hasn't actually eaten one for ages. She conjures up the words of her dieting counsellor: *You only have to want to be thin one per cent more than you want to eat the cake. Think of the future. Think how you want to look there. Take a breath. Say no.*

Little Chloe smiles and waves her one gloved hand at Ritzi as her mother drags her pushchair backwards towards the newsagent's. The dog is still straining to pull Bernie towards the park.

On the coach, Miss Hunter is wondering what Calum and Rahil are up to, hidden behind the seats in front of them. She can't see Josh, who is also hunched down, tearing through the plastic wrapper to get the drinks out for his friends.

On flight GX413, Dorothy Long, the woman sitting alongside the troublesome passenger, looks anxiously at the flight attendant. Why is the man taking no notice of her? Is he dangerous?

Across the aisle is a family of three, who were kind enough, during the flight, to take a look at Dorothy's baby pictures. Their child, a small girl of about five, has been charming for most of the journey, though a bit noisy and whiny at times. Over the course of the flight she has insisted on swapping seats with each of her parents, and now she's on the aisle. For some time she's been kicking the back of the seat in front of her but, hearing the tone of the flight attendant's voice, she stops. 'Why is the lady cross?' she asks her mother. Even she has started to sense the concern focused on the man in seat 42A.

TOCK

40 seconds to go . . .

Terry Potts, still on the phone, is trying to distract his friend from his problems by describing how the bike ran into the old lady. He's exaggerating a bit. He knows she wasn't actually hit. His picture of the cyclist will be spot on though, if unsurprising: tight Lycra shorts, hairy calves, dark glasses, and a pointy helmet decorated with flames. Terry uses a bike to get about, but he hates fanatics like this bloke, who give cyclists a bad name.

Marco turns in the direction of the clattering valve. He can hear the crucial washer rolling away in the direction of a gap in the floorboards under the tumble dryers. He'll look for it as soon as the customer is out of the way.

The digger driver lowers his scoop into the trench. Barbara Lapsom's opposite number, driving the car at the head of the queue facing the church, is seventeen-year-old Kelly Viner, who passed her test only a week before. Like Barbara, she is wondering whether, or when, to move forward. She's blaming herself for the traffic jam. Kelly had a feeling, when the temporary lights turned green, that the road ahead was blocked by the digger, but she didn't dare disobey the signal. Now she's no idea what to do: the lights are behind her, point-lessly changing colour while the road ahead is blocked. Surely the drivers queuing after her can see her problem? They can, but they're all (including the taxi man, who doesn't really want to move yet) sounding their horns in frustration.

Lorraine Lee has reached the bus stop halfway up the hill. Her legs are aching with the climb. A flash of temptation penetrates the *Scan-ner* mantra. She could sit on the bench in the shelter for a little while – just a couple of minutes – long enough to get her breath back. But she mustn't, not if she's going to be ready for the marathon. She must resist the urge to take a break. She kicks against the slope again. *Scan-ner.*

In the coffee shop, Juliet Morgan is trying to be just as strong – trying to focus on how bad she will feel in twenty minutes' time if she eats something forbidden. But before she can say no, the girl asks her again:

'Perhaps a piece of shortbread or some cheesecake?'

'Breathe! Eight.'

Charmaine and Chenelle are doing hand jives in time to the physical jerks in the studio and the rhythm of their own cheeky song. Miss Hunter reckons it's something she can ignore.

Bernie shouts to the workman, 'My letter!' pointing at the envelope in the hole, as Matey shrinks his body back down and slips into a Scottish accent, so the other man in his story can explain why he's unhappy: 'Pete said, "I've just . . ."'

TICK

39 seconds to go . . .

'"... seen the doctor."'

'And one . . .' Though the girls on the coach have picked up the timing, most of the women in the dance studio haven't settled into the beat yet. Maggie is repeating the exercise. She's only thirty but, though fit, she looks older. Her halo of frizzy curls, pink tie-dye headband and whopping hoop earrings are a little out of date. Exercise has been her lifeline since she dropped out of university, and she made teaching it her profession six years ago. She knows the science behind it – how the body releases its own happy chemicals when under physical stress – and she can see from her clients' faces that some of them are in desperate need of those chemicals today. She'll let her ladies relax and gossip after she's put them through their paces, but for now, though sympathetic, she must be tough. They may be miserable – desperate to get back to bed after broken nights with fractious babies – but she knows she can give them the ammunition to face the day ahead. Like Lorraine on her run and Juliet in the coffee shop, Maggie is investing in the future: what's a little pain now compared with contentment then? You can't live for the present all the time. She knows her ladies will be grateful to her when the class is over.

The architect outside lines up another shot. Deanna looks at her watch, even though she's only seconds away from the coffee shop, and the slight delay caused by letting him take his pictures is hardly going to make any difference. But she's desperate to see Paul. Maybe that wasn't him she saw in the distance. Or perhaps he's already in the café waiting, and wondering whether she is going to turn up.

Kelly Viner can feel tears coming. Everyone seems angry with her, and she doesn't really understand why, or know what to do. She was ecstatic when her parents gave her a car for her birthday. She'd always thought it would bring freedom and independence, and in some ways it has. How else could she be doing what she is now – making her own way to a university open day? But she is still a new and nervous driver, and here, at the front of the line of traffic, she is suffused with embarrassment. The poor people behind her might be in a hurry. They may have planes or trains to catch. She can't bear the idea that she is holding them up. If it goes on much longer, she might even be late herself, and for all she knows the university might make a note, and reject her when she applies. And she so wants to get in. It's said to be the best veterinary course in the area. She's always adored animals, and the idea of a lifetime spent looking after them is all that's keeping her going through the A-level slog.

Mariam turns off the bath taps, ready for another try at attaching the hose.

Noel Gilliard changes the font of the piece he is composing.

Setting off towards the church door, the vicar spots some confetti left over from a wedding at the weekend. It's banned, of course, but people still throw it, and it never seems to decompose, no matter how hard it rains. Hardly appropriate for a funeral; even less so than the sign painting, probably. He'll have to pick it up.

Matthew Larkin dips his brush in the paint again. Nearly finished. Then, when he's put the ladder away, he'll be ready to set off for the airport to meet his daughter. He's almost embarrassed by the joy that is building inside him. He knows what she looks like now, of course. They speak on *Skype*, and she sends photos in emails, but he still imagines her as the freckled-faced little girl with a kind heart and natural talent for art. That's what first took her to New Zealand: her painter's eye for the special light. Her paintings are rather different from his, he chuckles to himself, looking at the one straight red line he has completed over several months. It's just an ordinary sign here in Heathwick High Street, but in her world of galleries and dealers, his work might be considered avant-garde!

Over the road, Paul finally gets to his feet, handing the rescued change to Lotte, who is profuse in her thanks.

The taxi driver decides to go ahead with his illegal manoeuvre into the petrol station. He's sure his passenger will spot him there, and confident that he'll make the effort to find the cab, since it contains his extensive, expensive-looking luggage. Up ahead, he can see that once he's in the petrol station and in front of the digger, he'll be able to turn right onto the main road beyond the obstruction. Then the chances are that he'll have a clear run all the way to the airport. His passenger will be pleased with him for finding a way out of the jam. He might give a pretty good tip, too. He's obviously got money. Just look at those leather suitcases. He doesn't need to travel light. Maybe this run to the airport won't turn out so badly after all. For the first time since the traffic stopped, the taxi driver smiles.

The clash with the cyclist has interrupted the flow of the charity fundraiser's patter, and now Mrs Wilkins is distracted from her shock by the sight of her neighbour, Gillie Dougall, wading into the traffic with a large white box. Mrs Wilkins wants to know what's inside, and shuffles towards the road. She had intended to be feeding the ducks in the park by now, but one thing after another seems to be holding her up on her progress down the hill. Still, it doesn't matter. She's in no hurry.

On the coach, Josh starts handing round the cans. Calum and Rahil are still hunched over the mobile phone. They're watching a YouTube clip of a woman with her dress stuck in a car door. Calum is beginning to feel better. Before, all he could think about was what a prat he would look when he opened up the hopeless packed lunch his mum made him this morning: stale-bread Marmite sandwiches followed by stale-bread jam sandwiches with no butter, and no drink. It's the sort of thing Gran would make herself in the middle of the night. Maybe she has. Maybe, when he opens his lunch box, it will smell of wee, like her.

The workman takes no notice of Bernie, and carries on examining the pipe. In the newsagent's, the backpack man is digging into his pocket for the money to pay for his battery. On the petrol station forecourt, the delivery man has still not noticed the leaky pipe. And on flight GX413, in seat 41D (in front and to the right of the kerfuffle), Daniel Donovan, a retired policeman who had intended to sleep on the flight, but was prevented by the noise from the family behind him – and the child's regular kicks against his back – turns round to see what the fuss is about. He catches the moment when the look on the attendant's face passes from politely suppressed annoyance to alarm, and his old professional juices start to run.

TOCK

38 seconds to go . . .

As Nick tries to keep Mrs Wilkins' attention ('Madam! Madam!' he cries, though with her back turned she can't hear him), the cyclist, mumbling self-righteously, wheels his bike a couple of metres further on, to lean it against the lamppost outside the pet shop. There, Kate is trying to find the end on her roll of tape so she can stick up another sign. The cyclist hadn't intended to stop in Heathwick, but now that he has, he might as well check the bike over, and maybe pop into the newsagent's to buy an energy drink and a paper.

'Must dash,' Gillie Dougall mouths at the old lady. She feels guilty that she doesn't give more time to Mrs Wilkins, though she often does her shopping, drives her to the doctor's, or drops in for a chat. She's watched her decline over the past twenty years from a spry widow into a doddery pensioner, and can imagine how heart-breaking it must be to lose your friends and physical faculties as the years pass. But life is always so busy, even now that the children have moved out. Nevertheless, Gillie promises herself to take more care of her elderly neighbour after the party is over. She might even pop round this evening, if she can find the time, to apologize for any noise. Or maybe she should invite Mrs Wilkins to drop in? After all, the chances are that she won't actually come. But suppose she does? A new seam of worry opens up. Gillie doesn't want to upset her seating plan by adding to the numbers at such short notice. Her brow furrows as, holding her precious cake box tightly, she picks her way through the traffic towards the car park entrance.

There, the row over the badly parked van is intensifying, with Gillie's husband, Anthony, nagging Constable Lewis to do something, and the policeman urging Matey to stop talking so he can hear what Anthony is saying. The beggar's still in Scottish mode, telling of Pete's trip to the doctor: 'He says, "I've got . . ."'

Ritzi responds to Chloe's wave with a lurch towards the buggy. She can smell the damp rusk that lies, forgotten, in the folds of the blanket across Chloe's legs. Bernie is almost pulled off-balance by the sudden tug on the lead.

Lucy instinctively speeds up her backwards progress towards the newsagent's.

On the coach, the first drinks can is opened with a loud hiss.

The taxi driver looks in his mirror. He catches sight of the policeman, but can see that he's preoccupied with the crowd around the white van, and probably won't notice the cab mounting the pavement for a few metres.

'. . . and two . . .' The women in the dance studio are stretching alternate arms towards the ceiling.

TICK

37 seconds to go . . .

The cyclist debates for an instant whether to bother to lock his bike while he pops into the newsagent's. He decides to be cautious – after all, it will only add a few more seconds to his journey, which has been interrupted anyway.

'". . . a rare disease."' Matey rolls the 'r' on rare.

Bernie, relieved to see Mrs Wilkins moving in his direction with her potentially useful walking stick, calls her name and raises his hand to wave at her, forgetting that he is holding a plastic bag heavy with dog mess.

'Are you OK?' the girl serving in the coffee shop asks Juliet, who has been standing silent for five seconds. The waitress can't know the battle that is going on in Juliet's head about whether to yield to the temptation of a few moments' pleasure, or to keep her eye on the future, and say no to the offer of a cake.

Over by the window, Max is squeaking '*Beep! Beep!*' in time to the reversing signal from the digger. His mother is busy helping Polly, Lily and Nell stick the glitter onto their snowflakes and, without looking up, she shouts 'Ma-ax!' once again, unaware that her fellow customers are more annoyed by her constant, ineffective repetition of his name than by the child's harmless enthusiasm. Max takes no notice, as usual.

The flight attendant decides to tell the captain about her misgivings. She turns to walk back up the aisle towards the intercom.

'. . . and three . . .' Maggie's hands swoop to the floor.

Charmaine and Chenelle, still singing, do their best to copy her in the limited space they have available.

Calum and Rahil roar with laughter as the car in the YouTube clip starts to move, taking the woman's dress with it, and leaving her standing in the road in her underwear. There's another click, a hiss, and a spurt of foam flies across the aisle, hitting Kayleigh on the side of the face.

TOCK

36 seconds to go . . .

Matey has reached a key point in his joke, and tries to make eye contact with the little group around him. He almost whispers Pete's shocking news: '"There's no hope."'

Mrs Wilkins sees Bernie waving his bag of poo. Already smarting from Gillie's apparent rebuff, she takes it as an insult, and gives Bernie an angry stare.

Led by the carriage driver, who has put away his sugar cubes and reached up to grab one of the leather reins, Dime and Dollar start plodding their way up the alley, pulling the magnificent hearse. At the wheel in the little Mini behind the school coach, Sally Thorpe sees them coming, and realizes that even though she's reversed to let the undertaker slip through, the gap is too narrow for the horses, who will need plenty of space to turn into the road. She looks in her mirror. There's a long line of traffic behind her now. She can't go backwards, not even by the few metres that would make room for the funeral procession to nose its way into the queue. Sally knows it's not her fault that she's blocking the coffin's passage, but, like Kelly, she can't help feeling guilty. Why won't the traffic up ahead move forward? With the coach looming in front of her, she can't see.

Juliet smiles as she replies to the waitress. 'Oh yes . . .' she says, meaning that she's OK. The waitress, misunderstanding her, reaches for a plate. It's torture.

'. . . and four . . .' For some of the women in Maggie's class, the exercise is torture, too.

The vicar bends to gather up the confetti. He feels a familiar twinge in his back.

The cyclist takes a massive lock out of the pannier on the back of his bike. It looks almost as heavy and expensive as the cycle itself.

As Kayleigh shouts 'Miss!' the boy who sprayed her with his drink lets out a huge burp.

TICK

35 seconds to go . . .

'Who was that?' shouts Miss Hunter, as the children on the coach laugh, or do mock belches themselves. She knows she won't get a response from the culprit. Rory Lennahan stares menacingly at Kayleigh as he munches his crisps.

'. . . and five . . .'

Matey fixes on the undertaker with the next line of his joke, deepening Pete's Scottish voice still further: '"I'll die tomorrow!"'

Bernie lets the beggar's tale wash over him. Lowering his poo bag, he calls again to the old lady, hoping to sound more polite. 'Excuse me, madam!' he yells.

Although there is hardly any space behind her, Sally Thorpe puts her gear lever into reverse, hoping that the white lights on the rear of her car will signal to the next driver that he should move back, and set off a chain reaction down the hill.

The waitress in the coffee shop still thinks Juliet wants to eat. 'What will it be?' Juliet is staring at her laptop, hoping the sight of the dress will motivate her to turn down the offer of food. Only thirty-five seconds before she must place her bid.

Lorraine, the runner, has passed the bus stop. The hill is getting steeper now. She can feel it in her ankles, calves, knees and thighs, but she concentrates on the thought of her hot chocolate reward, pumps her arms, and forces herself on. *Scan-ner.*

In the plane, the passenger in seat 42A is still muttering. Dorothy Long in 42C thinks it might be some sort of religious chant. Her stomach tightens as her mind races across the possibilities. But what can she do?

As the cyclist attaches his lock, he spots the sign on the lamppost. Kate has found the end of the tape, and is tearing off a strip with her teeth, ready to attach another to the pet-shop window. She's thinking about her boyfriend, and how proud he will be when she tells him what she's done. It was Jon who introduced her to the animal-rights movement, and he who has persuaded her to come here today. He explained to her why he couldn't undertake the mission himself, and she agrees: it's important for him to stay underground, co-ordinating the efforts of others. He's too important to risk being caught on CCTV. Last year he was arrested at a protest near Cambridge that turned nasty, and he might be recognized. Jon reckons he's being watched by the police or the security services (which Kate finds achingly glamorous), and the two of them have set up a system of code words to make their texts, emails and conversations sound purely romantic, and not about direct action at all. For Kate, at least, the romance and the action are inextricably linked. She's proud of her warrior lover, though she has told only her closest friend the truth about the cause that's at the heart of their relationship (and sworn her to secrecy about what they plan to do).

Upstairs, Terry Potts looks at his watch, and shudders when he sees the time. He tries to find a gentle way of getting his friend to end the call, but only gets as far as a timid cough.

TOCK

34 seconds to go . . .

Kayleigh Palmer shouts out the name of the burper: 'Dominic, Miss Hunter!' As she speaks, something oblong flies over her head, and is caught by a boy facing backwards in the seat in front of her. Kayleigh thinks it might be a packet of cigarettes.

'What's all this?' the cyclist calls out to the girl by the pet-shop window. Kate turns. The small circle of face exposed by her balaclava glows with defiance. She's expecting – even hoping for – an argument. She's got half an eye on the policeman down the road, and she intends to be well out of the way before he comes up this end of the street, but she can't resist the chance to talk about how much animals mean to her.

Kate hadn't thought much about animal rights before the night in the pub when she'd first seen Jon, hunched,

125

mean and moody, over his pint, wearing the very coat she's got on today. Until she got to know him, she wouldn't have imagined herself capable of taking a stand about anything. But he has completely convinced her of the rightness of his cause, and she's prepared to do whatever it takes to stop vivisection and the commercial trade in innocent creatures. She wants to protect the animals, and she wants to protect Jon, too. And she doesn't fear the consequences for herself, whatever they might be.

Bernie's dog, Ritzi, seems to be only too aware of her rights, and she thinks it's time she was in the park. But Bernie wants to get his letter back. In a mixture of shouts and strange, one-armed sign language, he tries to explain to the distant Mrs Wilkins how he might fish it out of the trench with her stick. The old lady looks baffled.

Matey continues his story, not sure who, if anyone, is listening, but changing his voice back to cockney, just in case someone is following what is going on: 'Jack said, "Pete . . ."'

The undertaker gives him a smile.

The policeman looks across the road and sees the horses coming. He'll need to help them find a way into the traffic stream. He steps away from Anthony Dougall and the white van.

'. . . and six . . .'

The vicar, bent double like the women in the dance studio, collects up confetti from the church path.

TICK

33 seconds to go . . .

Anthony Dougall, furious that Constable Lewis has lost interest in his plight, follows him into the road towards the horses, still shouting about the need to move the van.

He doesn't see his girlfriend, Sharon, walking across the car park towards the little motor scooter she uses to get about town. Her eyes are red with crying, but she has to get on with her day.

Anthony's wife, Gillie, now in the middle of the road with her cake, has still not spotted him, though he's on her mind. She's feeling sorry for poor Anthony, stuck in a boring airport lounge on his birthday, no doubt with a stack of paperwork to plough through. She flips in an instant through worries she's nursed since the idea of a surprise party first came to her. Will he be angry? Too tired? Delayed? She's done everything to make it easy for him when he gets home. She's laid out a clean set of clothes, polished his shoes, bought smart new cufflinks as her birthday present to him. And yet so much could still go wrong . . .

'Thank you, Kayleigh,' says Miss Hunter, wishing she hadn't asked about the burp. She knows that, though there's no one sitting next to Kayleigh, someone in front, behind, or across the aisle from her will take revenge on Dominic's behalf. Like everyone else, Miss Hunter finds it difficult to like the girl: not very bright, unattractive without being ugly enough to evoke sympathy, and with that interfering mother who's a parent-governor now (since no one else wanted to do it). But Miss Hunter thinks she should protect Kayleigh Palmer, or at least be seen to try, and not just because Mrs Palmer is down in the street, monitoring the slow progress of the coach. For Miss Hunter has an inkling of what it feels like to be the most unpopular girl in the class. Indeed, one reason why Kayleigh makes her so uncomfortable is the constant reminder of scenes from more than twenty years ago, when girls held their noses as she approached, excluded her from their games at playtime, laughed whenever she did something wrong, and scoffed when-ever she got something right.

Mariam has connected the rubber hose to the bath taps.

She's ready to wash her hair. She wants to look good when she visits the university later today. It will be her second meeting with a research fellow who specializes in the politics of her homeland. She was put in touch with him by a compatriot in the kitchen at the hotel, and instinctively feels that he is someone she can trust. She wants him to find out what's happened to her family since she fled the country. She hasn't dared make contact with them directly, for fear that they would be punished, or that she might be traced. But she can't bear to live in ignorance, and so she's taken a calculated risk. She's had to reveal her real name for the first time since she entered the country. One casual slip by this new acquaintance, and there could be trouble. But it's worth it. Perhaps, today, he'll have good news at last. But even if the news is bad, any information will be better than not knowing. The morning is dragging. She can't wait for two o'clock. She joins in the song again.

Through the wall, Noel Gilliard curses, and accidentally deletes the four words that had made it onto the page in a brief moment of concentration.

Carefully balancing her computer, Juliet puts up her free hand to fend off the offer of cake. 'No. Thank you,' she barks at the waitress with a smug inner smile, relieved that, despite temptation, she's taken the long view, and is trading passing pleasure for lasting health and happiness.

'. . . and seven . . .'

In the dance studio, several of the class are regretting their decision to do the same, and wishing they were in the café eating pastries, rather than forcing their muscles to bend and stretch against their will.

'Good for you!' says the cyclist, praising (and slightly disappointing) Kate, who is psyched up for a challenge, not encouragement.

Bernie's pantomime continues, as does Matey's joke. '". . . that's awful but . . ."'

Sharon spots Anthony Dougall's car, and – amazed that he's still in Heathwick – starts walking towards it.

A mourner is coming through the church gate, striding towards the vicar with his hand out for a greeting. The vicar stuffs the confetti into the pocket of his cassock.

Now that he's on his feet again, Paul wants to get on his way to meet Deanna at the café, but Lotte, having thanked him for picking up her money, is talking about his scarf. 'Beautiful, but dangerous,' she says, fingering the rainbow knitting that Deanna produced as an early present, in honour of Paul's love of a long-gone Doctor Who.

The taxi mounts the pavement to its right.

TOCK

32 seconds to go . . .

A gust of wind blows a grain of grit from the roadworks into Gillie's eye. With both hands on the cake box, she can't rub at it, and she blinks furiously to try to get it out. In an instant her mind is running ahead. She'll have to face Anthony's guests with a bloodshot eye. And a photographer's coming. She'll spoil the picture that might be the key to him winning or losing the election. If he loses, it will be All Her Fault.

Lorraine can feel a rivulet of sweat running down her back. The phone in her tracksuit pocket is vibrating again. What if it's something important? What if something has happened to one of the children? For an instant, her rhythm is broken, but now it's back again: . . . *ner*. She's nearly at the top of the hill, and surely it won't hurt to wait a few seconds to see who wants to talk to her. But no. She's made herself a promise. She must go on.

'". . . don't be down . . ."' Matey is sounding like someone from *EastEnders*.

'. . . and eight.' The more reluctant exercisers relax, hoping their first burst of activity is over. But Maggie is determined to keep up the pace. As she speaks she drops gracefully to the ground, ready for the next sequence of stretches.

Having handed over the wreath, Janine is on the way back to her shop. She can see a group of people on the pavement outside. It's Kate Daintree, the cyclist and the charity fundraiser, but at this distance they all look like possible customers to Janine, and she presses on, regretting leaving the shop unattended. Half her mind is on her mother, too. Janine has locked her in the sitting room above the shop. For her own good. To stop her wandering.

As four more (specially shaken) drinks cans spurt open and bathe the coach's upholstery in sticky liquid, Miss Hunter goes to stand by the driver to watch the children in his mirror, just in case any harm comes to Kayleigh. Dominic is taking a bow. Janine's son, Calum, has surfaced from behind his seat to find out why everyone else is laughing. His half of the earphones drops out as he catches sight of his mother alongside the coach. It's clear she hasn't registered that it's come from his school, or that he's on board.

'Miss!' shouts Kayleigh, who is tempted to undo her seat belt so she can stand up and get the teacher's attention, but is afraid of getting into trouble if she's not strapped in.

With two wheels on the pavement and two in the gutter, the taxi will have to be quick if it's going to get past the digger before it swings round and blocks the way again.

Lotte and Paul see the cab coming, and squeeze themselves against the bakery window to avoid being hit.

Brow-beaten by the traffic behind her, Barbara Lapsom is too embarrassed to stay still any longer.

TICK

31 seconds to go . . .

Watching his mother from a distance, Calum realizes, for the first time, how anxious and tired she looks. He's suddenly sorry that he left the house in a strop about the pathetic packed lunch she'd assembled at the last minute. He decides to use his pocket money to buy her a present if there's a shop at the theatre.

'On the floor,' shouts Maggie, effortlessly completing the transition herself as most of the class, with creaking knees, stumble and totter down for the leg-lift exercises.

Following Barbara's lead, traffic starts to trickle from beyond the church down towards the shops. They're glad to be moving at last, but her first instinct was right: filling the space is only going to make the logjam worse, and more difficult to untangle. What's more, she gets a shock when the taxi unexpectedly comes the other way. She's surprised they don't scrape each other as she inches forwards and he darts by.

The baker dives towards the door of his shop to see what's going on. Old Lotte is one of his favourite customers, and he's worried that she's been startled by the sudden appearance of the taxi on the pavement. Joe Harman is the third generation of his family in the trade, and he's run the business single-handed since his father retired with arthritis ten years ago. His parents are upstairs now. It's a big day for them. Sheila Harman has finally decided to give up her work helping at a special needs school five miles away. She loves the children, and they love her sense of fun (and the titbits she brings in every day from the bakery), but David isn't getting any younger, and she feels the time has come for them to spend more time together before it's too late. Today the school is having a special assembly to say goodbye, with Mrs Harman and her husband as their special guests. They'd meant to leave by 9.15, but David can't find his car keys. They're looking in all the usual places. It's a scene they've played out many times in their long married life. 'Ask Joe?' says Sheila, sensing that, as so often these days, they are going to end up borrowing their son's car.

The story of Jack and Pete limps on. ' "I'll take you . . ." '
Matey has now latched onto Anthony Dougall, who is
furious that the policeman has deserted him to look after
the hearse. Anthony's got the general drift (it's something about two old friends, one of whom has a terminal
disease; the other is trying to cheer him up) but he's not
really interested. He looks up and down the street,
hoping to see the van driver returning. He doesn't
see Sharon making her way towards his own car behind
him.

On the plane, Daniel Donovan looks round again –
back and across the aisle. The woman in seat 42C
doesn't speak, but the two vertical creases between her
neatly plucked eyebrows deepen, and her eyes seem to
send out a mystified plea for help.

TOCK

30 seconds to go . . .

'Plenty of time,' says David Harman, with his hand down the back of the sofa, looking for his car keys. He doesn't want to admit defeat and borrow Joe's car yet.

As she expects, Barbara can't get past the digger, and she stops, sharply, bringing a new chorus of car horns from behind.

Leading the cars coming in the opposite direction, Kelly Viner, driving alone for only the second time since she passed her test, is panicking. She thinks everyone is blasting their horns at her, but she can't see what she should do. It's too late to copy the taxi – his illegal route through the petrol station is now blocked by all the cars that have come the other way. She edges forward, as close to the digger as she can get. It feels good to be moving, but now she's really trapped.

The taxi driver pulls up at the petrol station, glad that he made his move before the oncoming traffic blocked the road. The forecourt is empty, except for the tanker truck, making its delivery of petrol. It's giving off quite a smell. The driver, transfixed by the sight of old Matthew painting the sign over the road, has left everything switched to automatic, knowing that his pump will cut out when the underground stores are full. He still hasn't spotted the leak, and it is tiny, but a puddle of fuel is forming beneath the pipe.

At this short distance from the noise of the roadworks, it's easier to hear the funeral bell tolling its solemn message that a life has come to an end.

'Keep going!' Maggie nags, exercising to the rhythm of the music. Her movements are just as regular as the bell, but she's going at twice the speed, and her pulse speaks of life, not death.

Kayleigh's mother smirks through the glass at the shambolic performances of some of her fellow parents. She can't take her eyes off them, and has forgotten all about the school coach behind her. If she'd looked up, she might have been able to see the boy behind

Kayleigh slipping his hand between the seat and the window, ready to grab and yank her long frizzy yellow hair. Kayleigh's still shouting, 'Miss, miss.' She wants to tell Miss Hunter about the cigarettes.

In the launderette there's a toxic, gassy smell, even worse than the fumes in the petrol station, because the door is shut and there are no windows to let in fresh air.

Outside, at the mouth of the alley between the launderette and the dance studio, Dime and Dollar have come to a standstill. Their warm breath is turning to plumes of white vapour as they wait, obediently, for the signal to walk on. The children towards the back of the coach can see them, and shout to their friends who are sitting further forward to come and have a look. But the departure of the taxi has made a space in front, and the coach rolls along to fill it, so only the boys in the very back seat can see the horses now.

PC Lewis is gesturing to the traffic behind the coach to continue, backwards, down the hill, but no one seems to understand what he means. Frank, the funeral director, has got interested in the beggar's story and, seeing that there's nothing he can add to the constable's efforts to make way for the hearse, he reckons a few seconds spent waiting for the punch line won't hurt. Clutching the wreath in one hand, and waving his cane with the other (in sympathy with the policeman), he stays close enough to hear how 'Jack' intends to raise the spirits of his dying friend:

'". . . out for the . . ."'

Lucy can't hear Matey any more. In her quest for the second missing glove, she's managed to get herself and the pushchair to the other side of the van, and is now trying to open the newsagent's door with her bottom.

The vicar shakes hands with the mourner who just came through the lych gate. After the distraction of failing to get Matthew Larkin off his ladder and avoiding a fusillade from Ben Whatmore, he has forgotten the name of the deceased. He tries to start a conversation where it will become obvious. The day hasn't got off to a very good start. Surely things can only get better.

Other mourners are still puffing along up the High Street, glad that they abandoned the bus, but concerned that they won't make it to the church in time. The sight of the hearse blocked in by the traffic is both appalling and consoling for them.

One of them recognizes an old friend coming out of

the coffee shop. He waves, and shouts a cheery greeting across the street.

Her eye watering now, Gillie Dougall's panic level is rising with every step. The prospective catastrophes are mounting. You'd be amazed how short a time it takes to imagine a hundred things that might go wrong with a chocolate fountain, or to make a mental list of the insuperable consequences of being seen to fail in a social gathering composed entirely of friends.

On the plane, Daniel Donovan undoes his seat belt. The passengers around him recognize the metallic click, and turn towards him with reproving glances.

TICK

29 seconds to go . . .

The few children on the coach who have strapped themselves in undo their seat belts, so they can run back to see the horses. Only Kayleigh stays buckled up.

Daniel Donovan rises from his seat. The flight attendant has her back to him as she makes her way to the intercom. Daniel's a little unsteady, having failed to resist the free drinks trolley every time it passed. Something in his old police bones tells him that the difficult passenger is a terrorist, planning to bring the plane down. He's determined to do something to stop him, though he's thinking on his feet— Oops! Not quite on his feet.

'". . . time of your life."' Matey draws breath, ready to shift back into his own voice.

Still using the driver's mirror to watch the children, Miss Hunter missed Kayleigh's hair being pulled, but she has heard the summons to see the horses, and she wants to forestall a stampede to the back of the coach. She makes her gargling noise again: 'Guuuurrrrrr 8C!'

Lying on her side in the dance studio, Maggie is trying to impose some discipline, too: 'Lift those legs!'

Kayleigh's mother notices that Maggie's got a ladder in her tights, smirks, and sniffs again.

The wife of the cheery mourner nudges him in the ribs and hisses her disapproval at his unseemly behaviour in the street.

The digger starts to move to one side, but it's no help, because the road is now completely blocked with traffic coming from both directions.

Having learned the Highway Code so recently for her test, Kelly Viner knows very well that it's illegal to use a mobile phone when driving. Nevertheless, sweating, and breathing so hard in her panic that she's steaming up the windscreen, she reaches across to the passenger seat for her bag, so she can ring her dad to ask him what to do.

Sheila Harman decides to warn her son that she and David might need to borrow his car. She leans over the banisters leading down to the bakery, and calls out, 'Joe!' But Joe is out on the pavement now, making sure that Lotte is all right.

Halfway down the hill, the driver of the public bus has understood the policeman's semaphore, and starts to inch backwards.

Stuart Penton, panic-stricken about the split in his trousers, is still walking away from the traffic jam, up the hill, and out of Heathwick. He's beyond the petrol station now. He looks down at his feet. His other shoelace is undone.

Lucy can hardly get the newsagent's door open. The backpack man and Stefano from the launderette are at the counter, and the two fat ladies have stopped just inside the entrance, at the lottery ticket stand. 'Hello again,' says the shopkeeper, as the back of Lucy's head comes round the door.

As Deanna waves from the other end of the street, trying to let him know she's on her way, Paul is deep in conversation. Lotte, the old actress who dropped her change, is on about a famous dancer called Isadora

Duncan, who was strangled in the 1920s when her fashionably long scarf got entangled in the wheel of her car. 'You were lucky,' she says, wagging her finger at Paul, who sheepishly wraps his own scarf round his neck a couple more times, to stop the ends dangling down to his feet.

TOCK

28 seconds to go . . .

The remaining passengers on the public bus are furious now, as they feel it moving the wrong way.

At the exercise class, a few of the mothers are still getting themselves down onto the floor. Maggie is already lifting her left leg towards the ceiling. 'And one . . .'

Lucy smiles. 'Forgotten something?' says the newsagent.

Outside, the beggar is using his own voice again, describing the grand night out enjoyed by Jack and Pete: 'They saw a show . . .'

Sharon is closing in on Anthony's car. She's noticed, now, that the driver's door is open. Odd. Is he inside?

At the front of the eastbound traffic, Kelly Viner presses 4: her dad's number on speed-dial.

Terry Potts tries again to end his call so he can get off to work. 'Sure,' he says, interrupting his friend's flow. 'I must . . .'

Downstairs, having been ignored by Kate and the cyclist, Nick, the charity worker, has swooped on Janine, the florist. It's a double disappointment for her: the people outside her shop are not customers after all, and now one of them is trying to persuade her to give money away. 'A moment for the poor?' he shouts over the noise of the drills.

Stuart is debating whether to risk bending down again.

At the back of the plane, as she lifts the handset of the intercom to speak to the flight deck, the attendant turns and spots Daniel Donovan on his feet. Her terse cry – 'Sit down, sir' – carries a note of concern that spreads throughout the cabin.

There's a little bit of panic upstairs at the bakery, too. Sheila Harman calls again: 'Joe!'

But Joe is still outside on the pavement, listening in to

Lotte's story of Isadora Duncan's scarf calamity long ago.

Miss Hunter's cry has temporarily stopped the rush to the back of the coach, but it was just a moment's freeze. One girl braves it, and now almost everyone is out of their seats.

The postman stops his cart at the door between the shoe shop and the dance studio, right by the coach. He can see that things are getting pretty lively on board.

TICK

27 seconds to go . . .

At the petrol station there's now a steady trickle of fuel onto the forecourt, but the delivery driver is still watching Matthew, and the taxi man is tracking his passenger's progress at the cash machine.

'. . . and two . . .' Legs go up in the dance studio (almost in time to the music).

Bernie, still trying to signal his needs to the old lady, tunes back in to what Pete and Jack got up to on their great night out: '. . . went to a . . .'

'Dropped a mitten,' says Lucy, looking down on the floor for the stripy pink glove, knitted by her mother-in-law only a week before. Lucy could do without this delay. She's already going to arrive at Mrs Noble's house later than promised, and she knows from experience that she's in for some martyred sulking and snide remarks. She should be well away from here by now, but she knows she's got to find the mitten. Being late will be bad enough, but it will be even worse if young Chloe arrives with one cold hand.

Staggering across the aisle of the plane, Daniel Donovan is not sure what he's hoping to achieve. He rests his arm on the back of seat 42C and asks Dorothy Long, 'Are you all right?'

Terry Potts' friend keeps on talking, so Terry stays at the window. He sees Gillie Dougall with her cake box trying to find a pathway between the cars. She looks upset. He consoles himself with the thought that perhaps money doesn't buy happiness. All the same, he's not looking forward to finding out what *lack* of money can do.

Exchanging platitudes with the mourner outside the church, the vicar can't quite catch whether the dead man was called Ron or Don.

Meanwhile Stuart is balancing the risks of appearing at his interview with a loose shoelace or an even bigger split in the seat of his trousers.

TOCK

26 seconds to go . . .

'Please! One moment . . .' says Nick, as Janine sets about rearranging the tubs of flowers outside her shop. She doesn't want to be rude, but she can't bear to look him in the eye. She knows he's got to do his job, but she has no money to spare, and his presence can only drive away trade.

It looks like more fun on the other side of the road, outside the baker's, where Lotte is re-enacting the Isadora Duncan scarf disaster with flamboyant gestures worthy of a silent film. Joe, the baker, is watching with an indulgent smile, unaware that his mother is calling him again.

Janine's mother is calling too. Janine knows she is, even though she can't hear a thing. The old lady shouts for

Janine constantly, but does not recognize her when she appears. Secretly, Janine longs for the day when a physical illness ends her mother's mental turmoil, and Janine and Calum can start to live their own lives at last.

'. . . fantastic restaurant . . .' Matey speaks as if he has experience of the sort of place the two friends visit on Pete's final night out.

Lucy is stuck just inside the newsagent's door, behind the two women who entered the shop just before her. They are sisters with matching large rear ends. They're bending over to rest on the low shelf of the lottery stand, and can't help blocking her way into the narrow aisle. A garish poster above their heads shrieks that it's a Double Rollover, with an estimated jackpot of twenty-three million pounds. Lucy can't blame them for wanting a chance of winning that. Funny to think that a quick decision to stop and buy a ticket might change your life completely. Maybe she'll get one herself. She suspects that Chloe's mitten fell off beyond the lottery stand, near the parenting magazines, where she paused for an illicit read on her way round the shop earlier. She'd been scanning an article about 'The Terrible Twos' while twenty-three-month-old Chloe bellowed in her pushchair – desperate to get hold of a strand of tinsel dangling just out of her reach.

Lucy is amazed that Christmas decorations still have any impact on Chloe – after all, they've been up since September (four months: more than a sixth of Chloe's life!) – but now they are working their magic again, and Chloe is reaching out towards a display of chocolate Santas near the door. Lucy can't get past the women. She can't go round the other way, by the counter, because Stefano is standing there opening his cigarette packet, and the man with the rucksack is paying for his battery and some matches. For the first time, Lucy notices his foreign accent.

Up in the air, the woman in seat 42C nods towards the young man by the window. His eyes are closed now, and he's still chanting under his breath. *He's got a phone*, she mouths at Donovan.

'. . . and three . . .'

Things are getting very smelly in the launderette.

Bottom or shoe? Stuart ponders, convinced that his decision will mean the difference between success and failure at his interview.

TICK

25 seconds to go . . .

Daniel Donovan has read about phones being used to set off bombs. He knows that, though everyone's luggage has been scrutinized, the cargo hold may be full of commercial parcels that haven't been checked so thoroughly. Any one of them might include a detonator waiting for a signal from a mobile, and now they're over land on their descent to the airport, an explosion in the air would wipe out not just the people on the plane, but anyone hit by the debris below. If the man in seat 42A is a terrorist, he has to be stopped. Daniel must act. He reaches towards the oblong shape in the chanting man's shirt pocket.

The tale of Pete and Jack painting the town continues: '. . . ordered up all . . .' Looking down the hill, Matey sees Lorraine Lee, determinedly slogging towards him up the incline, her arms pumping, her head bobbing from side to side. Her strained face shows all the commitment of the serious runner. She's hurting, but in a few moments she will be able to stop for her wonderful chocolate drink, and that rush of contentment that Maggie knows her exercise class could experience, too, if only they would put in a bit more effort.

'. . . and four.'

The coach bounces to a stop, and some of the children topple over in their race to the back. Miss Hunter flips her hair, and makes her noise again: 'Guuuurrrrrr 8C!' but she knows she's done it too often today, and her powers of control are on the wane. She's taught some difficult classes in her time, but this bunch of undisciplined and ungrateful idiots are the pits. Do they really believe that she doesn't know what they are getting up to? More likely they don't care. She doesn't know why she bothers, and deeply regrets being persuaded by the headmaster to stay on for another year at Heathwick School. She was quite frank with him when she went to resign in July – she'd never much liked teaching, anyway, and only stuck with it for the long holidays – but he was already in trouble for losing too many staff too quickly and, with a mixture of flattery and bullying, persuaded her to come back in the autumn. She didn't have anything else lined up anyway, and for a brief but decisive moment she believed him when he said that things would look different after the summer break. But this will definitely be her last year. With any luck, she might be able to swing things so that this is her last school trip. If she doesn't make a move now, she'll end up as one of those bitter old teachers marking time on the way to retirement. Sometimes she feels like that already, though she's only thirty-six. Flicking her hair behind her ears yet again, she looks across to the dance studio ('. . . and four . . .'). How she envies the women who have the time to lie down and wave their legs in the air while she has to feign interest in Shakespeare yet again. Will she ever be like the pregnant mother with the pretty little toddler she was watching a minute ago?

Juliet Morgan stands in the café with her mug in one hand and her laptop balanced on the other. She's struggling not to spill her coffee, or let the lid of her computer shut. If it does, she will be cut off from the Internet just seconds before the auction ends. It looks as if a table may become free just in time: the mourners are squeezing between the tables and pushchairs on their way to the door. Max is still at the window: '*Ith wiverthin. Beep . . .*'

'Sorry. I'm busy,' says Janine, pulling a few wilting leaves off some chrysanthemums, and still not looking up at Nick.

At the cash dispenser, the taxi passenger looks at his watch.

And up the hill, Stuart Penton practises walking backwards with dignity. If he's sure he can leave the interview room without revealing the state of his rear end, it will be worth tying his shoelace.

TOCK

24 seconds to go . . .

On the plane, the chanting man grabs Daniel Donovan's wrist. The flight attendants at the front of the cabin, who had strapped themselves in for landing, unbuckle their seat belts.

'. . . and five . . .'

Ritzi is still pulling. She wants to go to the park, but she'd settle for the biscuit in the pushchair. Bernie yanks at the dog's lead while Matey carries on talking about Jack and Pete's night of excess: '. . . they could eat.'

Young PC Lewis, rather to his own surprise, has got the cars to copy the bus by reversing, and at last there is space for Sally Thorpe to move her Mini back a little. A gap is opening up between her car and the back of the coach. The carriage driver steps ahead of Dime and Dollar, ready to lead them out into the road when the space is wide enough for the hearse to come through.

In the café, Juliet inches carefully towards the empty table.

Miss Hunter is flicking her hair behind her ears again, still pondering the future. Maybe she should just drop everything – do something bold for once. She doesn't have to waste her teaching experience; she could go somewhere where her efforts will be appreciated – where people want to learn. She'll look on the Internet tonight for volunteer programmes and opportunities abroad.

Someone else on the coach is thinking about the future. Jeff Quinn sits alone, behind two girls who are writing other people's initials on the plastic armrests with felt-tip pens. He's reading a martial arts magazine. With his floppy fringe and gap-toothed smile, he's more popular than Kayleigh but, like her, he feels different from the other kids in the class. He's got an ambition – an obsession, some would say – to get into the British judo team. His dedication to his sport marks him out from the rest of 8C. Over the years, he's faced his share of ridicule (mainly from Lenny Gibbon), but the fact that his passion is judo, and not something like bird watching or archaeology, is a wonderful protection against the bullies.

The teachers sometimes give him a hard time, though. Last term, Mr Quinn was hauled up before the head for taking Jeff out of school for a judo masterclass in York. Apparently the 'unauthorized leave' made the truancy figures look bad. But why an extra bout of sport was worse for him than yet another day of ineffectual and disrupted lessons was a mystery to Jeff, and to his parents. They took the line that he'd be better off building up a skill that came naturally than straining to hear a supply teacher attempting to explain algebra over the Heathwick hubbub.

Jeff has already done some training before school this morning, and eaten the perfect breakfast to set him up for the county junior trials tonight. It's the biggest contest he's been involved in so far, and his whole body is humming with a mixture of excitement and nervousness. He knows there will be talent scouts there, and some of the best trainers in the country. Maybe one of them will offer to take him on. He'd been reluctant to come on the theatre trip, but his father didn't want to get into more trouble, and anyway thought it would be the best thing to take Jeff out of himself in the build-up to tonight's event. But so far nothing has driven from Jeff's mind the possibilities that lie ahead of him. For months he's been waiting for today – picturing by turns triumph and humiliation. He's imagined the weight of a medal around his neck, and an article in the local paper comparing him to the young diver who won gold at the World Championships. He'd love to be famous, and there's no way he can see himself getting into the news for anything else.

In the newsagent's, Stefano from the launderette is pulling faces to distract Chloe from the chocolate. With her dark hair and bright eyes, she reminds him of his sister's child. He's in no hurry to get back to work over the road. He doesn't know that his father, Marco, is desperate for his return. He's getting quite worried about the fumes now, though he can't show it with a customer in the shop.

TICK

23 seconds to go . . .

Marco writes out a ticket for the service wash. His eyes are watering because of the fumes. He knows it's unsafe to have the dry-cleaning machine in pieces, and he's not sure where the stopper for the valve ended up after it rolled away.

The vicar strides into the church to grab a copy of the Order of Service. He needs to check the first name of the deceased. He's ninety per cent sure it's Ronald, but pretty certain that the man he just met called him Don.

Nick, the charity worker, won't give up. 'Won't take long,' he says, sliding past Janine to block the way into her shop, so that she'll have no option but to stay on the pavement and listen to him.

Through her one good eye, Gillie Dougall sees them there. Janine is due to deliver the table decorations at 10.30. What if she's late? What if the order has gone missing? There's a funeral today – she's bound to be very busy. What if the traffic is still bad then, and Janine gets held up? Gillie had better check. She'll pop back as soon as she's got the cake safely into her car. If only she could get the grit out of her eye.

'. . . and six . . .'

Daniel Donovan instinctively swings his free hand towards the chanting man's chin. The flight attendant darts back down the aisle from the intercom to help her colleagues. In the cockpit, the co-pilot has heard enough to know that he should call for calm.

'Joe!' Sheila Harman still can't get a response.

'No hurry,' says her husband unconvincingly, as he explores the pockets of the jacket he wore the day before.

Outside the baker's, where Joe is out of earshot of his mother, Paul is too polite to stop Lotte's tale of Isadora Duncan's tragic designer scarf, even though he's finding the depth of her interest in the accident rather alarming. She's told him what the scarf was made of (silk), who designed it (some Russian artist Paul has never heard of), and what Isadora said when the car set off (*'Adieu, mes amis!'*). Now Lotte translates for Paul's benefit, gracefully swishing invisible fabric over her shoulder as she declaims, in a throaty foreign accent, 'Farewell, my friends . . .'

Deanna, seeing that Paul shows no sign of breaking away from the conversation, decides that if he's still talking when she gets past the photographer, she'll walk beyond the coffee shop to join him outside the baker's. The woman Paul's with has her back to Deanna, and she can't make out who it is. She hopes it isn't a relative or anyone he can't break away from. Whoever she is, she's acting in a very familiar manner – hanging onto Paul's arm, and speaking with her face very close to his. Surely Paul won't invite her to join them in the café? Deanna wants him to herself after so long apart.

The funeral director steps into the road, beckoning the horses into the line of traffic, but staying close enough to Matey to be able to hear what Jack and Pete are up to in his joke.

'They drank right . . .'

Dime and Dollar, as calm as ever despite the noisy drills and car horns around them, seem to sense that they are about to go on public display. They toss their heads, and lift their right forelegs in perfect unison. They are flawlessly groomed, their jet-black coats gleaming as brightly as the brass fittings on the complicated leather harnesses that attach them to the hearse. The driver, who will climb up into position as soon as he has led them out, carries a long thin whip, but he only needs it for show. Dime and Dollar trust him absolutely, and he trusts them. They can sense what he wants them to do from his tone of voice and the subtle tugs on their reins. He's been with them since he was a boy. He helped train them, and cared for them through the anxious time when work was scarce and it seemed that the family firm might not survive – which of course meant that neither would they. But then some film work had come along, a pop singer started a fashion for horse-drawn weddings and, as if by a miracle, on the very day the bank demanded a new business plan, Frank had enquired about hiring the pair to pull his special hearse.

It's been a happy partnership, and today Frank will walk in front of the procession with pride, knowing that Dime and Dollar will be at their best for him, as they are every time they come to Heathwick. They could do without the roadworks, of course, but Frank knows it will take more than that to upset these fine horses; and anyway, he'll be astounded if the workmen don't down tools when the fabulous carriage pulls onto the street. Once they're ready, he'll ask the policeman to clear the road up ahead, so they can set off, at walking pace, for the church.

Stuart Penton can't muster such a sense of decorum. He bends forward, raising his knee at the same time, in the hope of minimizing the strain on the seat of his trousers as he attempts to tie his shoelace.

TOCK

22 seconds to go . . .

Stuart topples over, onto something left behind by a dog whose owner was less scrupulous than Bernie.

Outside the bakery, Lotte continues in character, flinging out her arms and declaring: '*Je vais à la gloire!*' Paul knows what that means: 'I'm going to glory.' It all seems a bit far-fetched. He thinks it's unlikely that anyone would really come up with appropriate words on the point of unexpected death, but all the same, he and Joe, the baker, are enjoying Lotte's impromptu street performance.

Across the road, down by the newsagent's, Bernie's corresponding mime – trying to explain his plight to Mrs Wilkins – is still going on, but with much less finesse and audience appreciation. But Matey is getting more attention as he gets more lively, telling the story of the dying man and his friend painting the town: '. . . through the night.'

'. . . and seven . . .'

Marco's customer doesn't have the right money. Marco struggles to open his cash box to get change. The fumes from the dismantled machine are slowing him down.

Someone on the coach has farted. Charmaine and Chenelle are the first to smell it. They stop singing, and cry out 'Phowarrr!' in unison.

Juliet Morgan and Sam the barista are both making for the mourners' emptying table. Sam, with his anti-bacterial spray at the ready, wants to wipe it before she sits down. He's intrigued by the way she's clinging to her laptop, with the lid half open, as if she's in the middle of some important work, and desperate to crack on with it.

Mariam has mopped up the worst of the water, and is singing again.

At last, Kelly Viner hears a click, and then the sound of her father's phone ringing. It's taken only six seconds to get through, but it seemed like hours to Kelly, who would like to get out and walk away from the car. She wishes she'd never learned to drive at all.

Sheila Harman calls out to Joe again.

And the co-pilot of the aircraft switches on his microphone.

TICK

21 seconds to go . . .

Juliet would like a clean table, but she doesn't want to wait for Sam to do his job. She'll take the chance to grab the mourners' space before a plump woman with two children, who was in front of her in the queue but is still waiting at the counter for a selection of brightly coloured milkshakes and a piece of chocolate cake with three spoons. If Juliet doesn't get there first, she'll end up having to perch on a stool at the back of the café. There won't be much room there for her computer, and the auction clock is counting down.

Maggie thrusts her left leg higher up towards the ceiling. '. . . and eight . . .'

Noel Gilliard, annoyed by the thump of the bass from

the exercise class and Mariam's singing next door, pushes back his swivel chair.

Matey's story is changing gear: 'Next morning, hung over . . .'

Beside him, Anthony Dougall is trying to open the door of the white van. The policeman doesn't seem interested in getting it out of the way; he's totally absorbed in shepherding the hearse into the line of traffic. Maybe, if the keys are inside, Anthony will be able to move the van himself. If he's quick, he can shift it into the space that's just opened up. Whatever happens, he wants to get his own car on the move before the funeral procession pulls out in front of him. If he ends up stuck behind the hearse, there's a risk that his carefully planned deception will start to unravel. For now, he still has high hopes of pulling it off.

Just a few metres away, his wife is trying to balance his birthday cake on one arm, so that she can rub her eye, and maybe (discreetly) use her sleeve to mop up the wetness around her nose.

'Right, mate,' says Terry Potts, in his flat above the wedding shop, still trying to end his phone call, but to no effect.

'*Ladies and gentlemen . . .*' The co-pilot's calm voice fills the cabin, as flight attendants rush towards Daniel Donovan from both ends of the plane.

Stuart, still on the ground, is now in no doubt that the brown sludge on the left leg of his trousers is more than just mud. He's looking around for something to use to clean himself.

'It was deliberate?' asks Paul, engrossed in Lotte's tale now, and wondering whether Isadora's words about going to glory suggest that her death was suicide.

TOCK

20 seconds to go . . .

'I'm sure not,' says Lotte, obviously about to launch into a full explanation. Paul realizes it was a mistake to ask, and resigns himself to staying put a little longer.

Juliet takes a look at her computer screen. Twenty seconds left before she must press the button on her bid. She can see she's got at least two rivals for the dress. She reaches for her mug of coffee.

Maggie doesn't give her class a chance to relax. 'And one . . .' she shouts, starting again. She's keeping an eye on the sad new woman at the back, who's already sweating after only a few stretches, and seems to have problems sorting out her left from her right. Maggie reckons she can knock her into shape within six months if she comes every week, and she's thrilled by the idea.

It's what she loves about her job. But she can see that the woman is self-conscious, and not enjoying this session at all. She'll have a word in the water break, and tell her a little of her own journey to fitness – to encourage her to believe that exercise might change her life.

To think of it. Only a few years ago, Maggie didn't know what 'flex the foot' meant. That had been almost enough to drive her away from her first aerobics session, where everyone else seemed super-fit. If you'd told her then that one day she'd be running a class, she would have collapsed . . . with laughter.

She wants the new woman to look into the future and see this as the day that changed her life.

The door of the white van is locked. The beggar shrugs sympathetically at Anthony, while continuing his recitation: '. . . the dying man . . .'

Kelly Viner is still waiting for her dad to answer the phone in his office. She ends the call, and instantly dials again, hoping that he's got his mobile with him, and that he can tell her how to get out of this mess.

Scan . . . Almost at the top of the hill now, Lorraine has to dodge to one side as a motorbike mounts the pavement alongside her, to bypass the queue of traffic. She's lost her rhythm. She hasn't enough breath to say what she thinks of the rider and his female passenger, whose leather trousers look ready to burst.

The couple, Stan and Nina Krasinski, are on their way to their shifts as cleaners at the local hospital. They know that the agency they work for will cut their pay if they don't clock in on time, and that's why Stan is riding on the footpath. Too late, he catches sight of PC Lewis. In a split-second decision, he opts to speed up rather than stop.

In the shoe shop, Lenny Gibbon's mother is fed up with his wriggling, and gives him a quick slap.

Upstairs, Noel Gilliard rises from his chair.

'*Please remain seated,*' says the co-pilot on flight GX413, in the tone of a routine announcement. Nevertheless, someone at the front of the aircraft screams.

TICK

19 seconds to go . . .

Stuart's in luck. There's a large evergreen shrub to his left. It has wide leaves – perfect for the job. He rolls up onto his knees and reaches out to pluck one. Alas, it is just beyond his grasp.

'. . . and two . . .'

Noel Gilliard stretches up into the air, and sighs.

Matey's story has become rather touching. The dying man is grateful for his special night of fun: '. . . hugged his friend.'

. . . *ner*. Lorraine has got back in step, but the pause in momentum has given the pain in her muscles a chance to break through. And she can taste the bitter exhaust fumes left behind by the motorbike, polluting her healthy lungs.

Further up the road, Gillie Dougall darts out of the way of the motorcycle. Her sudden movement knocks the lid off her cake box and into the road.

Sharon has reached Anthony Dougall's car. She puts her head round the open door.

Terry Potts is no longer paying full attention to his friend on the phone. He's trying to plan what to say when he finally arrives at work. Looking down at the chaos in the street, he decides to use the traffic as an excuse, though the chances are that he could have got through on his pushbike if he had left earlier. This time he's firmer about needing to go. 'I'm sorry, mate . . .' he starts.

Behind the locked door of the cockpit, the flight crew know little of what is going on amongst their passengers. But when the cabin attendant rushed from the intercom to help restrain Daniel Donovan, she left the handset dangling, and it's picking up the sound of the scuffle. The pilot faces a decision. Should he abort the landing, and re-route the plane over a less populated area in case something happens, or get on the ground as soon as he can? On the open line to air-traffic control, his voice stays steady as he says, simply, 'We have a problem.'

As fumes fill the launderette, the fart is spreading through the coach, to outraged hilarity. Vinny McAlpine has gone bright red.

'Silent but deadly,' shouts Liam Tracy, alongside him.

TOCK

18 seconds to go . . .

Stuart is down again, and now his knees are muddy, too. He still hasn't done his shoe up, and the rip in his trousers feels longer than before. A golden career in journalism seems most unlikely now.

The cyclist and Kate, the animal-rights girl, are still talking. He doubts whether posters are enough to achieve change.

It looks as if Mrs Wilkins is going to come over to Bernie, so he stays put despite Ritzi's determination to get to the park. In any case, Matey seems to be getting to the meat of his joke. 'Choked up, he said . . .'

Lucy is still waiting to get past the gamblers. She should be at her mother-in-law's house by now, and she's anxiously craning her neck in the hope of seeing the missing mitten in the aisle beyond them. Despite Stefano's attempts to make Chloe smile, she is arching her back, trying to break free of her pushchair harness, and making an angry noise, just short of crying. She's stretching out towards the chocolate Santas that are just out of reach.

Lorraine's phone gives a short buzz. Someone has left a message. Lorraine promises herself that she'll stop to listen to it when she reaches the shops, and she needs all the motivation she can muster to get there. She focuses on the small group of people beyond the newsagent's, pretending to herself that they are the welcoming crowd at the finishing line of the marathon. *Scan-ner.* Almost there.

The architect is still taking pictures of the dance studio. Kayleigh Palmer's mother is getting suspicious. She's thinking of reporting him to the policeman over the road. Deanna wonders whether she should just push past him. She's fascinated to know what Paul and the woman are talking about so earnestly.

'. . . something rather different.' Lotte is explaining to Paul that Isadora Duncan's friends changed her last words, to make them more respectable than they actually were. He's at last spotted Deanna waving to him from outside the dance studio, and wants to hurry the tale along so he can run to meet her, but he can't deny Lotte the chance to complete her revelation of the truth about Isadora Duncan's death.

'. . . and three . . .'

Noel Gilliard sits down again – bolt upright in his chair, ready for serious work.

At the hat stand by the door of the coffee shop, the last mourner puts his arm into the sleeve of his overcoat. Juliet, glad that the mother who has ordered the chocolate cake is being served so slowly, sips her coffee and stares at her computer screen, watching the red timer count down.

Parked alongside the fuel tanker, the taxi driver is watching his passenger. It should be his turn at the cash machine any second now.

In the air, one of the crew has Daniel Donovan in a bear hug, pinning his arms to his sides. Daniel is still gripping the mobile phone, and shouting, 'No! Him!'

The man in seat 42A unbuckles his seat belt.

Alongside him, Dorothy Long puts her hands over her eyes. This can't be happening, surely? Perhaps she'll never get to meet her new grandson after all.

TICK

17 seconds to go . . .

'And she really said . . .?' prompts Paul, hoping Lotte will give a quick reply. But Lotte is repositioning herself, and adjusting her imaginary scarf, ready to re-enact her mime from the moment Isadora Duncan entered the car. It's like watching a film run backwards.

Stefano has taken a cigarette from the packet, and is trying to squeeze past Lucy to get out of the shop and back to the launderette.

There, Marco's customer comments on the fumes. Marco just wishes he'd go, so he can look for the lost valve on the floor.

Gillie dodges between the cars, trying to get her foot onto the box lid before the breeze blows it further away.

With her eyes on the road, she still hasn't noticed her husband, just a few metres to her left, or Sharon, who is now striding towards him from behind.

Matey has taken on the character of the dying man again, but there's a lilt in his Scottish voice now. He's happy. The night of wine, women and song has done just what Jack intended. Pete is full of gratitude: ' "How can I . . ." '

Max, the little boy at the window of the coffee shop, notices the hearse turning into the road. Bemused by the flowers on its roof, he stops mimicking the digger, and calls out, 'Mummy!'

'Not me. Him!' shouts Daniel Donovan at the crew who are trying to restrain him. He's staring at the man in seat 42A, who suddenly springs up and lurches over the woman in seat 42C, towards the aisle.

The child in seat 42D starts to cry.

'. . . and four . . .'

Mariam tests the temperature of her bath water. It's too hot.

Through the wall, Noel Gilliard stretches and bends his

fingers in the air over his computer keyboard, like a concert pianist limbering up for a performance at the Albert Hall.

The school coach is in uproar, with real and pretend farting noises, and Kayleigh Palmer shouting 'Miss! Miss!' as her hair is tugged from behind.

Miss Hunter is cursing herself for persuading Martin Knox, who should be the other teacher on the trip, to wait at his home by the ring road for the coach to pick him up. He was against the idea, but it seemed to her that it made perfect sense. On a normal day, it would have: their route takes them right past Martin's house, and they'd have collected him within five minutes of leaving school. Miss Hunter's plan meant that Martin could have some extra time to see to the needs of his disabled son, who has just come home after an operation, and she would be alone with the monsters of Year 8 for only a little while. Strictly speaking, it was against the rules, and Martin had been reluctant to stay at home, but Miss Hunter convinced him that no one would ever know. If only she hadn't made it impossible for him to refuse the offer. This traffic jam is bringing out the worst in Year 8. She could do with another pair of hands, or at least someone to share the ordeal.

TOCK

16 seconds to go . . .

The women at the lottery desk finish choosing their numbers. They stand up straight, pulling their bottoms out of the way of the door, and Stefano squeezes past.

Outside, Anthony Dougall has not yet noticed Sharon closing on him. He's calling out to the policeman again, annoyed that making way for the horses and the hearse is taking precedence over moving the white van. But his political instincts have not deserted him. He refrains from pointing out to the officer that the person in the coffin can't be in a hurry.

In the beggar's story, Pete is almost weeping as he thanks Jack: '". . . show my gratitude?"'

'. . . and five . . .'

Juliet stares at her screen. Sixteen seconds to go before her bid – an almost luxurious length of time. She tries to discipline herself not to click too soon.

Sam redistributes some of the chairs the mourners used. He didn't have the courage to tell them, but the manager doesn't really like more than four people round each table.

Alongside him, three-year-old Max, fascinated by the hearse, is still trying to get his mother to leave Lily, Polly and Nell, and join him at the window. 'Mummy!'

The florist is getting annoyed with Nick. He's talking about homelessness. She's sure she's seen the same boy before, raising money for something else. She takes her scissors out of her apron pocket.

Noel Gilliard breathes in, his hands hovering over his computer, ready to write something meaningful.

Mariam turns on the cold tap. The shower hose is still attached, and it dances round like a snake, spraying icy water everywhere all over again.

Dorothy Long, in seat 42C, surprises herself by punching her neighbour where it hurts.

'Oh grow up!' says Miss Hunter, reaching to open the window in the roof of the coach to let out some of the pong.

TICK

15 seconds to go . . .

Doreen, of Doreen's Dreams, is well on her way to the sorting office to collect the parcel she missed yesterday. Today, the postman has a delivery for Mariam. That's why he's stopped by the dance studio, alongside the school coach. Mariam's parcel is too big for her letter box. It's oddly shaped and badly wrapped. Whoever sent it hasn't paid enough postage, so he can't hand it over without collecting the difference. He rings the doorbell. Upstairs, Mariam, hit by the new jet of cold water, shrieks.

'If you ask me,' says the cyclist, leaning against the lamppost with his arms crossed, as Kate Daintree bites off another strip of tape.

Matey builds a tearful, drunken break into the voice he's using for Pete: ' "That was the perfect . . ." '

'Mummy!'

Concentrating on her laptop screen, Juliet can tell that she's going to find the child at the window really irritating.

As Stefano leaves the newsagent's, the customers shuffle around to take advantage of the extra space. The rucksack man hands over his money at the till. The lottery women let Lucy squeeze past into the aisle.

'. . . and six . . .'

The plane is filled with the sound of unbuckling seat belts, as passengers in the front of the cabin rise and turn to see what's going on behind them.

The man from 42A convulses in pain, collapsing across Dorothy's lap. He reaches down into the aisle to grab his phone from Daniel Donovan's hand.

And Stuart is on his feet again, at last. He gets to work with a leaf. It's not quite big enough to keep the muck off his hand.

TOCK

14 seconds to go . . .

A steward slams the side of his palm across the back of the man's neck. His body slumps. Dorothy Long, in seat 42C, feels his full weight pinning her in place.

The child across the aisle is shrieking now. Her mother says, 'It's OK, darling,' so unconvincingly that her husband, alongside her, has to reach for the air-sickness bag.

The voice of the co-pilot comes, deadpan, over the speakers once more: '*Ladies and gentlemen . . .*'

On the ground, Lotte Rabane has re-entered the imaginary limousine in 1920s Paris. She's Isadora Duncan now, and is blowing kisses to either side.

'. . . and seven . . .'

Noel's train of thought has been interrupted by Mariam's scream. He flops back into his chair, and wipes a non-existent bead of sweat from his forehead.

Mariam hasn't heard the doorbell.

The cyclist draws closer to Kate, and lowers his voice: 'There are times when . . .'

In the road, Gillie has her foot on the stray box lid, but she can't pick it up because her hands are full carrying the cake, which is simultaneously the source of complex worries and the repository of all her hopes. Gillie can do nothing about the pain in her streaming eye. If she drops the box now – or if she fails to retrieve the lid, and the cake gets covered in smuts from the roadworks, or rained on by the gathering clouds – her whole future might be threatened. Anthony's career could be ruined; and all because of her.

The optimism that had her singing in the shower just an hour ago is gone. Now her mind is staggering across a minefield of potential catastrophes – the worst disasters she can imagine, set off like toppling dominoes by her failures as a party planner: no one will turn up; there will be gatecrashers; not enough food to go round; far too much; Anthony teasing her in public about her red eye; whispered sneers in a corner about her shortcomings as a wife and hostess; the photographer taking unfortunate photos, and feeding stories about her hopelessness as a political spouse to the papers; electoral humiliation for dear, hard-working Anthony – just because he has a useless wife. Everything depends on the party working. That is why, now, the most important thing in the world is retrieving the square of white cardboard that is lying in the road.

Lucy spots the mitten, on the floor by the magazines.

Outside, Matey carries on: '". . . way to spend . . ."'

'Mummy!'
Max's mother stands up, still helping the girls with their useless scissors, and their tubes of glue.

At the florist's shop, Janine lifts some flowers out of a bucket and turns them over to snip their stems. Accidentally on purpose, water drips from them onto Nick's canvas shoes.

Outside the bakery, Joe catches Paul's eye. He shrugs and rolls his eyes to heaven as Lotte flicks the imaginary scarf over her shoulder a second time. Paul reads Joe's gesture as meaning *Crackers but harmless*, which more or less sums up his own view of the engaging old bird. At the same moment, they both hear Joe's mother calling from inside the shop.

TICK

13 seconds to go . . .

'Just a minute, Mum,' says Joe, who'd feel rude denying Lotte an audience of two for her magnificent performance. He can guess what's happened, and feels in his pocket for his own car keys. He's sure the school won't start their celebrations without Sheila, so there's no need to rush.

In the world of Jack and Pete, the drunken Scotsman is still showering his friend with thanks for making his last night on earth the best of his life: '"... the lascht day . . ."'

Over by the pet shop, Kate's face brightens as the cyclist continues: '. . . only direct action . . .' At last, someone who agrees with her!

Just a few metres from them, Kelly Viner, still worrying about how to get through the traffic jam, has at last got through to her dad. The first thing he hears is her squeal of fright as Gillie Dougall, her eyes wide with panic, plonks the cake box down on the bonnet of Kelly's car, so she can pick up the lid.

'. . . and eight.' The first round of leg-lifts is over. Half the class were relaxing on the count of seven.

'Mummy!'

Sam watches Max's mother walk towards the window. He's hoping she will take the boy away so he can give the glass a good wipe before the manager sees the state it's in.

With one hand supporting her pregnant tummy, Lucy bends to pick up the mitten. The movement makes her unborn baby kick again.

'Must go . . .' says Terry to his distraught friend.

On the street beneath him, the Krasinskis' motorbike has come to a stop, unable either to get through the traffic or, because of the digger and the trench, back up onto the pavement. Even if it could, Stan Krasinski would have a job finding a way past the florist and the charity boy, the animal-rights girl and the man with the bicycle. So the hospital cleaners are now stuck with everyone else. They are pretty sure they are going to lose some pay. What they don't know is that the policeman behind them is making a note of their registration number. They may be fined as well.

At air-traffic control, the trainee who has been assigned the task of handling what was supposed to be a routine landing calls for help.

'*Please stay seated*,' says the co-pilot. Two attendants are sitting on Daniel Donovan in the aisle. He's still protesting that they've got the wrong man, but they're holding his face against the floor, and it's impossible to make out what he is saying.

Dorothy Long is shaking with shock. The strange young man lying across her lap appears to be unconscious. But who knows what he was planning? Is there a timer ticking somewhere on the plane, ready to blow it out of the sky? Has he got accomplices elsewhere in the cabin? She wishes she could reach to get the picture of her grandson out of her handbag. If she's going to die, she wants the image of his innocent face to be the last thing she lays eyes on. But the body slumped across her means she can't move, and her bag has been stowed for landing anyway. She doesn't want to break the rules, and she doesn't want to make a fuss, so she sits and prays, for the first time in her life.

Stuart's praying too, and with equal lack of hope. Sweating now, despite the cold, he makes the mistake of pushing his hair back off his clammy forehead with his dirty hand.

'*Adieu, mes amis*,' Lotte repeats, even more passionately languid than before.

TOCK

12 seconds to go . . .

There's a thumping noise and a whirr from the belly of the plane. It's the normal sound of the wheels going down in preparation for landing, but it brings squeals of panic from some of the passengers.

'". . . of my life,"' says Matey, preparing to switch back to his own voice.

Outside the pet shop, the cyclist is jumbling the code numbers on his combination lock, still talking to Kate, the animal-rights campaigner: '. . . will achieve anything.'

'Don't worry . . .' she says, over his bent back, before he has even finished speaking.

At the coffee-shop window, Max is pointing at the

hearse. 'Mummy, why . . .' he asks.

'Other side!' Maggie is not going to let the exercise class lose momentum.

Lucy slowly straightens up, panting, and slightly dizzy, the mitten safely in her hand.

Gillie is bending down now, balancing the cake box on Kelly's car bonnet with one hand, and reaching for the lid on the ground with the other. It's too far for her to stretch without losing her balance.

On the kerb, only a few metres away, Sharon taps Anthony Dougall on the shoulder. The policeman closes his notebook. To Anthony's fury, he starts walking towards the Krasinskis' motorbike.

As Terry slips one arm into his overcoat, ready to make a dash for work, his friend launches into even more intimate detail of his troubles.

Too late, Stuart realizes that he now has mud, or worse, somewhere on his face, and possibly in his hair as well.

TICK

11 seconds to go . . .

The supervisor in air-traffic control walks towards the flustered trainee.

'. . . and two . . .' The regulars in the class know that Maggie is being kind. She's counting the lifts before some of them have even changed legs.

'. . . we've got that covered,' says Kate, slightly offended that the cyclist thought her commitment to her cause stopped at sticking up posters. There's so much more she could tell him, if Jon hadn't dinned into her the need for caution: *Remember. You never know who you're talking to.* Maybe she's already said too much. And now the policeman is looking in their direction. Should she run, or try to get Lycra Man to help the cause?

The florist steps towards her shop door. Nick blocks her way, desperate to get his first sign-up of the day. He's talking about regular payments – small donations that can do great good . . .

'Pub at six?' says Terry, hoping that will get him off the phone in time to save his job, while giving his friend a reason to keep going through the day.

Down the street, Matey takes on a portentous tone: 'But Jack was glum.'

Holding up the mitten, Lucy puts on her sing-song voice for Chloe. 'Here it is, darling,' she says.

Max's mother is trying to pull him away from the window, to join the girls with the glitter and the glue, but he tears himself out of her grasp, pointing at the hearse, and saying, 'Why's that box . . .'

More mourners arrive at the church, one of them carrying a stack of service sheets, fresh from the printers. He gives one to the vicar, who is back at the door, ready to receive the coffin. The leaflet is a gaudy affair, with a picture on the front of the dead man, Donald Whyman, raising a pint on a quayside. The vicar chants *Donald* in his head. Good job he checked. Now all he needs to do is find a way to get rid of the confetti from his pocket without being seen.

Watching from beside the diesel pump, where he's lifting out the nozzle, ready to fill up with fuel, the taxi driver is confused. His passenger is walking away from the cash machine. Surely there hasn't been time for him to get money out? The taxi driver shouts and waves, to show the man where he is waiting.

A few metres away, Lotte has paused for dramatic effect before revealing Isadora Duncan's real last words. She's tossing the phantom scarf in the air and showering kisses on an imaginary crowd of admirers.

'Joe!'

'Just a minute, Mum.'

Stuart has the idea of using the screen of his phone as a mirror, to see just how dirty his face is.

TOCK

10 seconds to go . . .

Stuart's pocket is empty. He looks down, and sees his phone lying screen-down in the muck.

'Problem on GX413,' shouts the trainee at air-traffic control.

The taxi passenger doesn't seem to be looking for the cab. He's going in the wrong direction, up the side road, away from the High Street, round the corner to the side of the church.

Matthew Larkin is still painting the thermometer sign. The vicar hopes the traffic will hold up the hearse and the family cars long enough for Matthew to finish his work and move the ladder before the widow sees it.

At the other end of the roadworks, Ritzi, the little golden cocker spaniel puppy, is more boisterous than ever, still tugging at the lead, and now jumping up on Matey, who keeps talking while patting her head: 'The dying man . . .'

And on her phone in the car at the head of the traffic jam, Kelly Viner is talking so quickly that her father can't understand what she is saying.

'. . . and three . . .' The exercise class is formed of two distinct groups now: those at the front, who are just getting into their stride, and those at the back, who are already struggling.

The postman rings Mariam's doorbell again, trying to deliver the parcel. She hears the bell this time, but she isn't dressed, and her pyjamas are soaking wet, so she ignores it.

Noel Gilliard has given up the idea of writing anything for posterity. He clicks the email icon on his desktop.

Downstairs, Lenny Gibbon is trying to untie his trainers, ready to have his feet measured. He says nothing, but it's clear that he's furious with his mother about the slap. He only just managed to stop himself hitting her back. It won't be long before he's bigger than her, and they both know it.

In the coffee shop, Juliet stares anxiously at the auction screen. The red countdown shows thirty seconds to go till the end of the auction. Ten seconds till she has to press the button to reveal her bid. She knows that some-where another woman has a maximum price in mind. It may be higher than hers, and all her plotting may be futile.

Inches away, little Max tugs on his mother's arm, and repeats, 'Why's that box . . .'

Terry is still trying to get away from his friend on the phone. 'You'll be OK?' he asks.

On the coach, only three children are quiet. One is Jeff Quinn. He's ignoring the mayhem all around him, and doing the word search in his judo magazine: looking for terms like *ippon*, *hansoku-make*, and *waza-ari*. He can't get his mind off tonight's contest – not that he really wants to. He can't wait for this theatre trip to be over, and to get into his judo suit, ready for the bout.

The second is Rahil, who is plugged into his sister's phone, and using the Internet at her expense.

The third is Calum, the florist's son, no longer wired

up, but counting his money, and thinking about the present he is going to buy his mum.

From outside the baker's, Paul gives Deanna a reassuring wave, as Lotte reveals the truth about Isadora Duncan's last words. She cocks her head to one side, and her French accent becomes even more luscious than before. '*Je vais à l'amour!*' she purrs.

TICK

9 seconds to go . . .

Lotte reaches forward and grasps Paul's hands, staying in character for the unnecessary translation. 'I'm off to love!' she cries, embarrassing and amusing him at the same time.

Relieved to be given the cue to get away, he waves down the hill to a bemused Deanna.

Stuart bends forward again. No more ripping. A small mercy. His trousers must have reached their limit. He picks up the filthy phone. The screen will be no use as a mirror now.

Rory Lennahan, who was never interested in seeing the horses, has finished his crisps now, and is blowing into the empty bag, ready to pop it. Two rows back, Shilpa Kohli is picking at the split ends of her long black hair.

Beside her, Melinda Hurst is filing her nails. Like Jeff, the judo boy, they are excited; but they're trying to hide it. They've both had enough of Heathwick, and they plan to break away from the class when they get to the theatre. Someone Melinda met on the Internet is going to meet them nearby. They've got money, fake ID and a change of clothes in their bags. They're not planning to catch the coach back.

The taxi driver calls out again to his passenger, who is disappearing round the corner by the pub. Flustered, he looks back at the cab. He's right. The luggage is still there. The cases alone are worth a fortune, never mind whatever is inside them . . . Whatever is inside them . . .

'. . . and four . . .'

'Why's that box . . .'

In the coffee shop, the chocolate cake woman has finally picked up her order: so many things that they've had to give her a tray. She's looking for somewhere to sit with her noisy children. Juliet pushes her laptop towards the centre of the table, to try to make it look as full and uninviting as possible.

'. . . couldn't understand.' Matey has one eye on

Lorraine. She has nearly made it all the way up the hill to the shops. Bernie cheers on her final, desperate, steps. Flapping and panting, she reminds him of Dr Roger Bannister finishing the first sub four-minute mile. In the black-and-white newsreel Bernie saw at the Saturday morning pictures more than half a century ago, Bannister had flailed and gasped like a seabird hit by a bullet, and collapsed on his friends waiting at the tape. Now Bernie holds his arms out ready to catch Lorraine. He accidentally drops Ritzi's lead, and the dog sets off at speed for the park.

'Seems OK to me,' says the air-traffic control supervisor, looking at the screen. His tone is deliberately calm, and the trainee gets the message: *Don't panic.*

Terry really must leave for work, but he's worried about his friend, and wants him to know it will be all right to ring him if he's in trouble. 'Mobile. Any time,' he says.

Outside the dance studio, the photographer lowers his camera, and Deanna slides past him, on her way to Paul at last.

'Joe . . .'

TOCK

8 seconds to go . . .

'Just a minute, Mum.'

Paul frees himself from Lotte's grip, calling out, 'And I am too!' He can see Deanna getting closer.

On the coach, Charmaine and Chenelle scream with laughter at the sight of Bernie and Lorraine's strange embrace.

A few metres away, the man who found the first mitten is rummaging through his backpack, inadvertently becoming part of Matey's audience. The tables have turned in the joke: the dying man is concerned about his healthy friend now: 'So he asked . . .'

The group around the beggar is growing all the time,

and it looks as if Mrs Wilkins will be joining them soon, too. At the edge of the crowd, Anthony gives a startled jump as he realizes that Sharon is beside him. Sharon moves in closer, calling out his name.

At the other end of the street, the cyclist has locked his bike, but still hovers close to Kate. She's seen the policeman coming in their direction, and knows she'd better make a move. But she's wondering whether she has a duty, for the sake of the cause, to keep talking to the cyclist. Meanwhile, Brian Eglington, the owner of the pet shop, has stepped outside to investigate the poster. He's recognized the girl who stuck it there, despite her attempt at a disguise. He knows that Kate is the daughter of Donny Daintree, the breakfast show host on the local radio station. She used to come into the shop every Saturday to look at the kittens. Donny Daintree's show is blaring away inside right now.

In her rear-view mirror, Kelly catches sight of the policeman too. She thinks he's making directly for her car. She's sure he's going to tell her off for using her phone, and drops it on the floor without turning it off.

'. . . and five . . .'

In the café, Juliet Morgan lifts her handbag onto one of the empty chairs at her table, hoping to keep the woman, her children, and her cakes away; and Max finally spits out his question: '. . . got flowers on it?'

'Not today, thanks,' says Janine, the florist, as politely as she can manage. She doesn't want to explain to Nick that she's going to need every penny she's got for Christmas, and beyond.

The taxi passenger strides purposefully away. He's picking up speed. The taxi driver's bemusement is turning into suspicion.

'Trouble in the cabin,' says the trainee air-traffic controller, flustered, but trying to keep the depth of his concern out of his voice.

Stefano is on his way back to the launderette. He's looking for his lighter.

TICK

7 seconds to go . . .

'Bravo!' Lotte laughs, as Paul strides away.

'. . . and six . . .'

Stuart's panic has brought on an urgent need to relieve himself. At last, some good luck. There's a large oak tree just a few metres away. He strides off towards it, only slightly impeded by his loose shoe.

Outside the newsagent's, the backpack man is unwrapping the battery he bought in the shop.

'"What's wrong?"' says Matey, putting on the voice of Pete, the dying man in his story.

'Ritzi!' Bernie shouts after the fleeing dog, but his cry is drowned out as a drill starts up again.

Sharon flings herself at Anthony. 'You can't leave me!' she pleads, convulsed in sobs.

Mariam tests her bathwater again. It's cool enough to get in. She starts unbuttoning her pyjamas.

Through the wall, Noel Gilliard is getting ever more irritated. It seems to him that the email link is taking ages to come up.

Marco is lying on his belly on the floor, reaching underneath the drying machines for the lost valve. His sleeve is picking up dust and grease. Obviously the new cleaning lady hasn't been mopping the nooks and crannies. He makes a mental note to tell her off when she comes in tonight.

'Give me a break,' says Nick to the florist. There's just a hint of a catch in his voice, and Janine realizes that he's probably just as hard up as she is.

Max's mother, still talking over her shoulder to her friends, giggles at his question about the coffin.

Juliet realizes she knows the woman with the three

spoons: it's Felicity Milner, a work colleague who never returned from maternity leave three years ago. *She's let herself go*, thinks Juliet; smiling, just in case Felicity recognizes her, too. There's no sign of a response.

The vicar sneezes.

Across the road, in the petrol station, the taxi driver shouts and waves, but his passenger either can't hear him, or chooses to take no notice.

'What sort of trouble?' the air-traffic supervisor asks the trainee.

TOCK

6 seconds to go . . .

'I'm not sure,' says the trainee air-traffic controller.

Paul is striding downhill towards Deanna, with Lotte still shouting after him: 'Watch that scarf!'

Anthony Dougall tries to muffle Sharon's declarations of love by holding her close to him.

'And Jack said . . .' It's the denouement of the beggar's joke. The healthy man is going to tell the sick man why he is miserable.

'. . . and seven . . .'

The architect has done as much as possible without actually entering the dance studio, and he can see that now would be a bad time to do that. He ponders whether to go back to his office or to grab a quick drink at the coffee shop.

The policeman has changed his mind. Much as he would like to deal with the motorcyclist, it's more important to get the traffic moving. He signals to Kelly to wind down her window.

At last, the webmail menu is on Noel's screen. He enters another password: *D1cken5*.

'Two minutes, then,' says the florist, tucking her scissors back in place.

Brian Eglington, the pet-shop man, is furious at the accusations on the poster. He tears it from the window, but instead of confronting Kate, he storms back into his shop. He's got a better idea of how to get back at her.

The taxi passenger breaks into a run.

The man with the backpack is still fiddling with his battery.

Lucy is too embarrassed to leave the shop without

buying anything. She stops at the counter and asks for a lottery scratchcard.

Max's mother shrugs her shoulders and rolls her eyes to the ceiling, as she yells across to her friends, 'What a moment . . .'

TICK

5 seconds to go . . .

'. . . to explain the mysteries . . .'

The air-traffic supervisor speaks sternly: 'Well, find out,' he says, listening across the line to hear how the trainee handles his first little difficulty.

Exhausted and embarrassed, Lorraine disentangles herself from Bernie. She is still fighting for breath. 'Just give me a minute,' she tries to say, knowing from experience that it won't take long for her to be back to normal, but all that comes out is a wheeze and a grunt.

Despite the confusion around him, Matey continues with his story, mainly for the benefit of Frank, the funeral director, who is trying to look as if he isn't listening while waving the hearse on. The beggar's changed his accent again. Now he's speaking as cockney Jack. His tone is full of hungover misery, grievance and self-pity: '"It's all right . . ."'

'A pound's worth of hope,' the newsagent says with a smile, as he takes Lucy's lottery money.

'. . . and eight.' Breathless, aching and humiliated, the new woman at the back of the exercise class has decided that she won't be coming back next week.

'Miss!' shouts Kayleigh on the coach.
     Miss Hunter flicks her hair behind her ears.

Kayleigh's mother is still watching the exercise class with contempt.

Six miles away, at the other end of the phone, Kelly's dad can hear her distant voice and the beeping of a reversing vehicle, but he can't understand what is going on.

The postman is annoyed. There's still no response from Mariam, and so now he is going to have to write out a card telling her to collect the package herself. It will take time, and these days everything he does is measured and monitored. If his deliveries take too long, he will be in trouble when he gets back to the sorting office. He reaches for his pen.

Deanna sidesteps the postman's cart. She's just a few metres from Paul now, and he is picking up speed, with Lotte's voice echoing behind him: 'Get something shorter!'

Preparing to send/receive says the message on Noel's computer.

Someone comes out of the shop at the petrol station, carrying a plastic fuel can. He is walking in the direction of the shops and the car park. The delivery tanker is still dribbling fuel.

The vicar rummages in his pocket for his handkerchief.

On the school coach, Rory Lennahan starts up a song: '*Why are . . .*'

TOCK

4 seconds to go . . .

'. . . *we waiting?*'

As Kate and the cyclist discuss the politics of animal rights on the pavement outside his shop, Brian Eglington is dialling her father's radio phone-in. He knows the number by heart. It's repeated constantly every morning, but until now he's always resisted the urge to call and vent his views on everything from immigration to capital punishment. But now he can't stop himself. He's going to reveal to that smug slug Daintree exactly what his daughter is up to, and he's going to break the news in public.

Bernie has a moment's indecision. He can tell from Matey's tone of voice that he has almost finished, and he's torn between running down the hill after Ritzi and staying to hear the end of the joke.

'"... for you ..."' The beggar pauses for a beat, hoping his listeners will be aghast that a fit man could envy someone who is dying.

'Good luck,' says the newsagent, handing over Lucy's scratchcard, and smiling down at Chloe, who is waving her gloved hands in the air.

In the coffee shop, Max's mother tries to prise her son's fingers off the window, but she keeps on laughing with her friend about her unexpected predicament of having to explain matters 'of life and death' to a three-year-old.

Lifting her mug of black coffee, Juliet Morgan smiles at the little boy's innocence, and wonders whether she will ever have babies of her own. Maybe her weight loss will help. Thank goodness she didn't give in to that cake.

At the back of the café, the chocolate-cake woman is struggling to lift her children onto high stools to eat their sugary feast.

The architect decides that, since the traffic is so slow, he might as well stay in Heathwick a little longer. He turns towards the coffee shop.

Terry Potts rests his head against the window, listening. He feels that his friend is now stable enough for him to be able to leave for work. He hopes he won't get into too much trouble for being late, but if he does, it was worth it. He might have saved a precious life.

Preparing to send/receive says the message on Noel's computer.

Confused to see his passenger rushing away, the taxi driver gets back in his cab. If he can find a way through the traffic jam, he'll chase after him.

As Stuart gets into position behind the oak tree, his phone rings. He automatically uses his free hand to lift it to his ear, spreading dirt across the side of his face.

'And lift!' Only seven repetitions to go.

The air-traffic control supervisor takes the trainee's microphone and calls out himself: 'GX413 . . .'

The vicar feels another sneeze coming on, and whips out his handkerchief.

Paul can't hear Lotte any more, but she is still shouting to him: 'We wouldn't want . . .'

The policeman hears a male voice calling from the foot well of the car: 'Kelly!'

Gillie Dougall looks up and sees Anthony and Sharon clasped in each other's arms. Suddenly all her imagined worries are subsumed into a real horror she never expected to feel.

TICK

3 seconds to go . . .

Confetti flies across the entrance to the church just as the mourners start to flood in.

'. . . and two . . .'

'Kelly!'

'Ritzi!' shouts Bernie, as the pup bounds on towards the park.

Lorraine's phone vibrates again. This time she reaches for her pocket.

Lenny Gibbon is struggling with a knot in his laces. His mother reaches down to untangle it for him. He pushes her away.

The hatred he feels for his mother is mirrored by the love drawing Deanna and Paul ever closer, as Lotte cries out her warning: '. . . something awful . . .'

The gas man is shouting, but no one is looking. No one can hear.

In the launderette, the fumes are making Marco quite woozy. He wishes Stefano would come back.

Stefano is crossing the road.

There is no way the taxi driver can get out of the petrol station to pursue his passenger. He looks back at the man's luggage – the big heavy bags he helped load up earlier. The man might be in a rush to catch his plane, but why would he abandon them?

A message from the plane comes into the controller's headphones: '*This is GX413 . . .*'

'Joe!' The baker's parents are still trying to attract his attention.

On the coach, more voices join in with the song: '*Why-aye are . . .*'

'Gotta go, mate,' says Terry Potts.

Down in the street, Matey echoes his words, grabbing the edge of Bernie's coat to hold him there as he reaches the climax of his joke. He's finishing with a cockney flourish: '". . . I've gotta go . . ."'

TOCK

2 seconds to go . . .

'"... to work now!"'

Bernie has missed the punch line of the joke. He's thundering down the hill in pursuit of Ritzi, almost as breathless at the start of his run as Lorraine was at the end of hers. His bag of poo swings from his fingers, twisting in the air as he runs after his dog.

'... *we waiting?*'
    Rahil has started the YouTube clip again. Calum still can't help laughing as the car tears the lady's dress away, but this time he's thinking of his own mother, and how awful it would be (for him as well as her) if she were the woman in the film.

Kate, the animal-rights girl, is fumbling in her bag.

Alongside her, the florist is trying to be patient, but wishing that she'd never let the charity boy start talking. She nods respectfully at two of the mourners as they make their way past. You never know. They might want to take flowers to the burial.

Seeing the shower of confetti, a mourner walking up the church path gives the vicar a filthy look.

Paul is out of earshot now. Lotte's last words are swallowed up by the digger: '. . . to happen to you!'

'. . . and three . . .'

From the floor of Kelly Viner's car, her father's voice calls out again, 'Kelly!'

Downloading message 29 of 33 . . . Noel can tell without opening them that all the emails are spam so far.

Max won't come away from the window. His mother yields, crouches by his side next to the glass, and ponders how to tell him about coffins and funerals.

Juliet, with a table to herself, steeped in pride at having resisted the cakes, and revelling in the relief of not being recognized by someone who has only known her as a fat slob, feels at last that her future may be truly happy. She moves her bag from the chair beside her just in case the smart gentleman who is just coming in needs a seat.

The asking price for the dress is inching upwards, but no one has yet bid as much as she is prepared to offer. It may really become hers in just a few seconds' time.

Across the road, Lorraine is bent almost double, with one hand braced on her knee to steady herself, while the other holds her phone to her ear. The person who has called can hear only traffic noise and heavy, wheezing breaths. It's Lena, one of Lorraine's original running buddies – one of the marathon dropouts – guiltily calling to see how she is, and to catch up on the progress of the scanner sponsorship drive. She'd meant to call earlier, to suggest that Lorraine should come over to her side of town so they could go for a jog together there. But Lena was distracted by something on the TV breakfast show. It was only when that awful cook came on that she'd got round to dialling Lorraine's number. Too late, obviously. Lorraine is already out training.

The postman pushes the card through Mariam's letter box.

'I'm trying to help!' snaps Mrs Gibbon.

Stuart's mother means well, too, when she says, 'All set, dear?' not realizing that her call has got him into even more of a mess.

And the baker's mother shouts out 'Joe!' once more.

The gas worker in the trench is waving furiously, unseen.

At air-traffic control, the pilot's voice comes across as confident and calm. 'We have a problem.'

Up his ladder outside the church, Matthew Larkin makes another paint stroke, carefully ensuring that he hasn't gone over the line. He wouldn't want to imply that the restoration fund is healthier than it really is. Out of the corner of his eye, he sees flight GX413 coming in from the east. Its wheels are down; the wing flaps set for landing. He wonders whether it's his daughter's plane.

'You take care,' Terry says, with feeling. He knows he's going to worry about his friend all day.

The passengers who got off the bus down the hill are congratulating themselves on their decision to walk. One has even decided that he's saved himself enough time to pop into the newsagent's to buy a paper. The crossword might come in handy if the address at the funeral is over-long.

'Not long now,' says another, whose wife, wearing tighter shoes than usual, has been wearied by the walk. They step over Matey, barely noticing that he is there.

'Just a second,' Joe the baker calls to his mother, giving Lotte a peck on the cheek.

TICK

1 second to go . . .

Frank, the funeral director, stifles a laugh, in case any of the mourners are looking. As he steps forward to pat Dime and Dollar, and to take his place in front of the hearse, he puts his hand in his pocket, looking for some change to throw to the beggar.

The horses nuzzle each other's noses, and the carriage driver swings himself up into his seat, ready to move off when the traffic clears.

'Whatever,' snarls Lenny Gibbon in the shoe shop, adding a mumbled, but audible, 'Cow!'

Stumped for a reply to his mother, Stuart switches off his phone.

Brian Eglington's heart beats a little faster as he waits for his call to the radio station to be answered. Any moment now, he will be able to make Kate's life a living hell.

As the church bell continues to toll, the mourners pick their way along the crowded pavement. They still have a hope of beating the cortège to the church. Serena Dunn, the deceased's long-suffering secretary, looks through the window of the hearse at her old boss's coffin, and refrains from saying the words that come into her head: *Late for his own . . .*

Gillie Dougall takes her foot off the box lid, and straightens up, holding the cake before her. Both her eyes are watering now, and her body has started to shake. Part of her brain is searching for an innocent explanation for the scene before her, but she knows there can't be one. Just an hour ago, Anthony told her he was about to board a plane in Salzburg. It's a two-hour flight. He was lying. There was no conference, and from the look of that woman (surely it can't be Sharon, who'd helped her plan the party, and advised her on what to wear for her photo as the perfect wife?), that wasn't the first lie.

Like the controller, the pilot is speaking with deliberate calmness. '*Trouble with a passenger,*' he says. The controller isn't sure what to make of that yet, but he pushes a button alerting the airport fire brigade to stand by.

'You're a marvel,' says Lena, humbled by Lorraine's commitment to her cause.

Yet again, PC Lewis hears the deep male voice coming from the floor of the car: 'Kelly!'
Terrified of being late for the university and in trouble with the police, Kelly is in tears now.

Send and receive complete. Definitely no fan mail then. Noel Gilliard shrugs and reaches out for someone who *does* think he's the world's greatest writer – indeed the world's greatest human being. Vita the cat, still curled up on the towel on the radiator, stretches out in her sleep.

Max's mother puts on a soft, earnest voice to explain the coffin to her son. 'Well, you see . . .' she says.

'. . . and four . . .'
One of the women in the fitness class spots her daughter looking out of the coach and gives a thumbs-up sign.
The girl, embarrassed, ducks out of sight.

The gas man in the trench is still shouting and waving.

Paul and Deanna raise their arms, ready to embrace. In just a moment they will be reunited. '*Je vais à l'amour!*' he cries, beaming with love.

'Shut up, you fool,' hisses Anthony Dougall, bending his head closer to Sharon's ear.

Shaking with fury and pain, Gillie Dougall dashes the birthday cake to the ground.

Mariam steps into the bath as, down in the street, the postman throws her package back into his cart.

Marco's son, Stefano, opens the door of the launderette and lights his cigarette.

Unaware of the puddle of petrol on the forecourt, the taxi driver turns on his engine.

The clock on Juliet's computer reads 09.21.59. Full of hope, she pushes the button to bid on the fabulous dress, just one second early.

Alongside her, little Max presses himself against the glass, his eye dodging between the twin attractions of the horses and the digger. His tiny friend Polly is still singing '*Likkle schtar . . .*' as she, Lily and Nell run towards the window to show him their glittery snowflakes.

As Lucy Noble starts rubbing at her scratchcard, Chloe pulls off one of her mittens and drops it on the floor.

'Please don't go!' says Terry's friend.

The vicar drops to his knees to clean up the confetti. And Matthew Larkin presses the lid back onto his paint tin.

'Just a minute, Mum!'

Flicking her hair behind her ears, Miss Hunter walks up the aisle of the coach. 'Guuuurrrrrr 8C!'

Rahil yanks the wire from his ear and quickly stashes the phone out of sight.

Rory Lennahan stuffs a sausage into his mouth to hide it.

Kayleigh Palmer shouts, 'Miss!'

Jeff Quinn doesn't notice any of the mayhem around him. He's still engrossed in his judo magazine. He's finished the word search and is reading tips on nutrition and exercise. He can't wait for tonight's competition.

And the boys in the back seat carry on with their song: '*Why are we . . .*'

TOCK

9.22 a.m.

EPILOGUE

Six months later

8.10 a.m.

RADIO PRESENTER: It's ten past eight, and you're listening to the Morning Newshour on Radio Heathshire.

It's six months now since the disaster that made Heathwick a household name, with the loss of sixty-five lives, many serious injuries, and the devastation of the ancient centre of the town.

Later today, the official Commission of Inquiry into what happened will publish its interim report on the tragedy. To find out what it's expected to say, I'm joined by my former colleague Donny Daintree, whose own daughter, Kate, was one of the victims. As many of you will know, Donny gave up his job here after the loss of his daughter to devote himself to seeking the truth about how she, and so many others, died.

Thank you for coming in, Donny, on what must be a distressing day for you and your family.

DONNY: I'm glad to be here and, of course, every day is distressing for us since we lost Kate.

PRESENTER: Indeed. I'm sure the listeners understand what you are going through, and we're grateful to you for coming back to your old studio today.

Now, you, and the relatives of other victims, have been pushing for the publication of this report. Tell us why.

DONNY: What we are hoping for is a clear picture of the sequence of events. You remember the chaos on the day. I was actually on the air when the first reports came in, and for a long time we weren't at all sure what had happened. Had there been one explosion or many? Was it terrorism? A plane crash? Something to do with the gasworks that were underway that morning? And why were the emergency services so slow to respond? I for one am haunted by the thought that my daughter might have survived if help had reached her sooner.

PRESENTER: And you're still in the dark about all this?

DONNY: Yes. With so many people who were

there either dead or seriously injured, it was impossible to get a clear account at the time. If anything, things have got worse since then, with news organizations and websites all over the world coming up with incompatible theories and dubious evidence. As you know, we failed to get the official Inquiry held in public. The government insisted on secret hearings because of the suggestion that terrorists might have been responsible, and the commercial sensitivities of the gas company and the airline involved. It means that we, the relatives and the injured victims, have been cut off from important information, and it may be months, or even years, before the Commission finishes its work. That's why I'm delighted that we have persuaded the Commission to bring out this interim report on the causes of the disaster – to put our minds at least partially at rest. It means we won't have to wait for the full report, which will go into much more detail, and include recommendations for action to avoid anything similar happening in the future.

PRESENTER: So, what are you expecting today's report to say?

DONNY: Well, I'm pretty sure it will bear out some of the things I and other researchers have found out through our own investigations. For example, we know now that there may have been as many as four explosions, set off in a sort of domino effect. But we don't yet know for sure which was the first, or precisely what caused it. I'm pretty confident that the Commission will resolve that this afternoon.

PRESENTER: And your best guess is?

DONNY: I think the blast that happened at the petrol station was the first.

PRESENTER: Yes, there was a fuel delivery in progress at the time, wasn't there? Did something go wrong with that?

DONNY: Possibly, and the oil company may have serious questions to answer about their safety procedures. But it seems that today's report may well reveal a more sinister explanation – something that hasn't been made public before. Now, your listeners will recall that a taxi – the only other vehicle on the forecourt at the time – was completely destroyed in the explosion and subsequent fire. It's my understanding, having talked to contacts in the Inquiry team, that remnants of explosive devices have been found amongst the remains of the luggage in that taxi.

PRESENTER: So this was a planned terrorist attack?

DONNY: Not necessarily. Or not a planned

attack on Heathwick, at least. As you know, the town is not far from the airport. It's my belief that someone was on his way there with deadly intent.

PRESENTER: So the terrorist died in the blast? It was a suicide attack?

DONNY: I don't think so. Remember, only three bodies were found at the petrol station – Charles Perry, the taxi driver, Keith Oxley, the driver of the petrol tanker, and John Hardy, who has been identified as the owner of a white van which had run out of petrol further down the street. There does not appear to have been a passenger in the taxi.

PRESENTER: So the taxi driver, Mr Perry, might be a terrorist suspect?

DONNY: There's nothing to indicate, from his history, or from what his family and friends have said about him, that he had any question-able views or associations. My theory is that he and his passenger were held up on their way to the airport in the terrible traffic that day. I sug-gest that the passenger knew that the timer in his baggage was counting down, and that he got out of the taxi to save his own skin.

PRESENTER: But why would the taxi driver have kept his luggage?

DONNY: Perhaps the terrorist said he was

coming back. As you know, the police have released some footage from the CCTV camera outside the bank in Heathwick High Street. Of course, that camera wasn't trained on the traffic – it was watching the cash dispenser outside, but at one point you can see a taxi door open, and shortly afterwards a man passes close by the ATM. That man has never been named, despite police appeals for him to come forward, and there are no unidentified male victims now. The one body they can't put a name to is definitely that of the beggar who had been a feature of the High Street for years. It's my belief, and I understand it to be the view of the police, that whoever got out of the taxi was the bomber.

PRESENTER: So you think he was on his way to the airport to catch a plane. But surely, with all the security there these days, he'd have been bound to be intercepted.

DONNY: But maybe he had no intention of getting aboard a plane. Perhaps he wanted to bomb the crowded check-in area – where he could position his luggage to do maximum damage before the security checks kick in. Surely the timing of the explosion – if it was set off by a timing device – suggests that he expected to be at the airport then. And he would have been if the traffic hadn't been so bad.

PRESENTER: So that's one explosion accounted for, and given that it was at a petrol station, it's not surprising that its impact was catastrophic. But you, and some of the survivors, say there were more. How do you explain them?

DONNY: Well, first, look at the pattern of damage. As you say, the buildings near the petrol station were bound to be affected, but right at the other end of the street, there was major devastation.

PRESENTER: That's where the school coach and the funeral cortège were hit?

DONNY: That's right. What seems to have happened is that the first explosion set off another. Remember, the reason for the traffic chaos was emergency gasworks in the High Street.

PRESENTER: You think there just happened to be an escape of gas as the first blast happened? That sounds a bit of a coincidence.

DONNY: It does. But one of the people in our victims' support group is convinced that there was trouble in the roadworks. Many of your listeners will know Bernie Blackstock, the manager of the Rose and Crown. He escaped death by a whisker, chasing his dog, who was running away. Bernie recalls one of the gas workers trying to raise the alarm in the seconds before the explosion.

PRESENTER: So that explains two blasts. You say there may have been as many as four. Why do you think there were others?

DONNY: Well, you'll understand that I need to protect my sources here, but I'm told that forensic evidence points to two other incidents, neither of which would necessarily have been so tremendously devastating on their own, but which were exacerbated, or perhaps even triggered, by the bigger explosions. One of them may have terrorist implications. There hasn't been any publicity about it, which of course makes it all the more interesting.

PRESENTER: And what is this forensic evidence?

DONNY: Well, a postman was making deliveries in the High Street at the time of the blasts. He was killed. It's my understanding that an examination of tiny fragments from the wreckage of his cart has revealed explosive damage on the inside.

PRESENTER: But that surely suggests a coordinated attack on Heathwick itself?

DONNY: My sources tell me that there is no similarity between the debris of the devices found in the taxi and in the cart. It seems that the postman was about to deliver some sort of parcel bomb.

PRESENTER: In Heathwick? That sounds a bit far-fetched. It's not exactly Baghdad or Belfast.

DONNY: I can't tell you how I know this, but it seems that shortly before the disaster a potential target had taken a room above the dance studio in the High Street. This is the 'unidentified woman' on the casualty list issued by the authorities. It's my belief that they know full well who she was, and are withholding her name for security reasons. I hope there will be some information about her in the report this afternoon.

PRESENTER: And the fourth explosion? Something set off by the other three?

DONNY: Perhaps not. I've been talking to a fireman who was on the scene soon after the disaster − he doesn't want to be named. He's mystified as to why one of the shops right at the end of the street suffered a total and cata-strophic collapse. It was across the road from the gasworks and well away from the other explosions. This was the launderette. Your lis-teners will probably remember it.

PRESENTER: It was flying masonry from there that killed the horses, wasn't it?

DONNY: Yes, that's one fact the authorities

have released to the press. The proprietor and his son died too. And it seems possible that this fourth explosion – if indeed that is what happened there – may have been caused by the build-up of inflammable vapours from the dry-cleaning machine. Obviously, on a normal day, that would have been a momentous event for Heathwick in itself. We may never know what actually happened, unless today's report reveals more evidence.

PRESENTER: Does it really matter what caused those particular deaths? If the Lorenzos hadn't died in that explosion, they might have been killed by one of the others.

DONNY: The fact that you ask that question brings home the sheer enormity of the overall event. Sixty-five deaths. Some of them possibly avoidable. It's not good enough to assume that this was a completely unavoidable fireball.

PRESENTER: Which brings us to your other main concern. The length of time that elapsed before the emergency services arrived on the scene.

DONNY: This is crucial. Official logs show that the first emergency call was made at nine twenty-four, and yet the first fire engine didn't arrive until nearly ten o'clock.

PRESENTER: Do you think today's report will

have an explanation for that delay?

DONNY: I think it will, and I think we already know what went wrong. Do you remember that day, when the news first came through? I think we all assumed, knowing that Heathwick is on the flight path, that such devastation could only be explained by an air crash – perhaps a plane in trouble coming down short of the airport. We were wrong. But it turns out that there *was* an air emergency that morning. A plane had radioed about a suspicious passenger and a fight on board. The local emergency services had been scrambled to the airport. You'll recall that the spending cuts last year involved the closure of Heathwick fire station and more sharing of facilities with the airport fire service. It was hoped that there would never be two major incidents at once.

PRESENTER: But fire appliances were not needed at the airport that morning.

DONNY: Well, as it turned out, that plane landed safely, but not until some minutes after the explosions in Heathwick, and the controller felt she could not release fire engines and ambulances from the airport until it was absolutely clear that they were not needed there. She followed procedures to the letter, and did not divert anyone to Heathwick until the plane had come to a standstill, and all the passengers had disembarked.

PRESENTER: With hindsight, she should have broken the rules?

DONNY: With hindsight, yes. It's hard for me not to criticize her when I know that my daughter was lying in the rubble needing help while firemen were standing by at the airport twiddling their thumbs.

PRESENTER: Of course, the people to blame for that were the people threatening to bring down the aircraft.

DONNY: If there really *was* a threat. That's another thing we're hoping today's official report will cover. The airline has been silent on this. Two men were dealt with swiftly at a magistrates' court before their connection with the incident was publicly known. Both pleaded guilty, and their cases went unreported. They received suspended sentences.

PRESENTER: Have you spoken to them?

DONNY: I've tried. One is a foreign national who was deported, and has disappeared. The other, a British man, is suing the airline, and refuses to speak to me while that case is pending.

PRESENTER: But you see him as in some way responsible for your daughter's death?

DONNY: It's hard not to, though I know there are others more directly to blame. The thing is, I know his name. It's easier to focus my anger on him than on any nameless suspect. That's why so many of the parents of the children who died on the school coach are angry with Martin Knox, the teacher who should have been with them, but wasn't. He's left the teaching profession now, by the way. We're all looking for somebody to blame.

PRESENTER: Of course, your daughter, Kate, was a suspect for a while.

DONNY: Those were my darkest days. Your listeners will know that the attacks on my family nearly broke me. I thought she was at school, but in fact she was distributing animal-rights literature in the High Street. Some of the survivors saw her doing it. They just assumed that she was to blame when the explosions went off.

PRESENTER: She was a militant?

DONNY: She may have fallen amongst dubious friends, but I have no reason to think that she was ever involved in violent protest. We have lost a dear, sweet diamond from our lives. I'm proud of her commitment, even though I don't agree with her, and I wish to heaven that she had gone to school that day.

PRESENTER: You have our sympathy.

DONNY: Thank you. It was a nightmare when she was under suspicion. But we're not the only family who suffered vilification in the press, and even on phone-ins to this station. Some survivors thought the white van I spoke about contained a bomb. All the evidence suggests that the driver, John Hardy, had simply run out of petrol at the wrong place at the wrong time. And perhaps even worse, one of the survivors, Farouk Osman, spent weeks in the burns unit surrounded by police officers waiting for him to come round. An eye-witness remembered his beard and his rucksack and interpreted this as 'acting suspiciously'. It turns out that he tried to save some of the children on the burning coach. Let's hope that his heroism is recognized in the report today.

PRESENTER: His actions are one of the few good news stories from those terrible events. Are there any more?

DONNY: Well, I think we were all cheered when Bernie Blackstock's puppy, Ritzi, who had saved her master's life by running away at the crucial moment, was found several hours later, safe and sound, thanks to an appeal on this radio station. And of course, there's the story of our new MP, Anthony Dougall, who lost his wife and a close colleague that day.

PRESENTER: Yes, indeed – that famous photograph of his birthday cake lying among the debris has become one of the iconic images of the disaster.

DONNY: He refused to be beaten by the experience and carried on his election campaign. I'm sure that, now he's in Parliament, he will fight for the full details of what happened at Heathwick to be made public in due course.

PRESENTER: And I hear he is happier in his personal life, too.

DONNY: Yes, he has just announced his engagement to one of our former colleagues, who has been working with him on a television film about the disaster, to be broadcast tonight.

PRESENTER: Congratulations to them both. And by the way, that film, *Heathwick's Day of Doom*, is on BBC One tonight at nine p.m.

And while we're plugging other people's programmes, I should mention a three-hour special on the disaster here on Radio Heathshire from six p.m. It's going to be presented by Stuart Penton, the young man who was on his way to a job interview at the *Heathwick Echo* when the disaster happened. As we know now, if the disaster hadn't happened, Stuart would have arrived to find a locked office. The Editor was late for work – miraculously escaping the total destruction of the newspaper's office, but also missing the biggest story of her career. Well, Stuart became a crucial part of the initial rescue attempts, and won all our hearts with his eyewitness accounts of what he saw that day. You all probably know that on the strength of that work he's become chief reporter for a national newspaper. He joins us now to tell us more about this evening's programme. Good morning, Stuart.

STUART: Good morning.

PRESENTER: So what do you have in store for us at six?

STUART: Well, too much to mention it all here, but we'll have full details of the Commission report, of course; along with profiles of the teacher and the ten pupils from Heathwick School who died, and interviews with the team of counsellors who have been working with the staff and children there, to help them with their shock and grief. I'll be talking to Dora Pilbury, widow of Frank, who has so bravely carried on the family undertaking business after her husband's death – arranging the funerals first of Frank himself, and then of many of the victims of the tragedy.

Some of the survivors will give us their

memories of the day, including people who, like me, had very lucky escapes. There's Doreen Talbot, of Doreen's Dreams bridal wear, who was lucky to have been called away from her shop just before the disaster. Some of you may have seen Doreen in a famous gossip magazine. She's become quite a celebrity. I'll be asking about those rumours that one of the cast of *EastEnders* has commissioned a wedding dress from her new shop. And the Reverend Jonathan Davis, who was such a hero on the day, will be telling us about the work that's going on to repair the stained-glass windows at St Michael's Church, which were blown out by the blast at the petrol station. That work, of course, is being funded in part thanks to the hugely successful auction of paintings by local artist Terry Potts, who died when the bridal shop collapsed.

The new bridal shop, by the way, is to be officially opened by the winner of *Britain's Got Talent*.

PRESENTER: All this national interest in Heathwick – and it doesn't end there. We've heard that the new edition of *Savage Firebrands*, the novel by our local author Noel Gilliard, who died in the tragedy, has reached the top of the bestseller list. What a shame he didn't live to see his publisher re-issue it.

Mr Gilliard's cat was never found, was it, Donny?

DONNY: No, and of course we still have the mystery of the true identity of the beggar who died outside the bank. I'm sure many of our listeners will recall how he used to sit there telling jokes and asking for money. Sad to say, it turned out that no one knew his real name.

PRESENTER: Perhaps that's something that will come out in the report of the Commission of Inquiry.

DONNY: I doubt it. There are rumours, you know, that he was a stand-up comedian back in the eighties. His stage name was Dan Moloney. Someone's put an audio recording of one of his old performances on YouTube. No one seems to know what happened to him since then. Maybe he's nothing to do with our 'Matey', and perhaps he's still alive. If so, the police want him to come forward so they can move on to other inquiries. Meanwhile they're asking anyone who might have anything with Dan Moloney's DNA on it to hand it in. They want to compare it with the DNA of the unidentified man. Perhaps if any of you have information on Dan Moloney, or the man who was known as Matey, you could ring us here at Radio Heathshire or send a text, a tweet or an email.

PRESENTER: You're doing my job for me, Donny! I'd better let you go before you ask me to give you back the microphone. Thank you for coming to your old studio to tell us what to look out for in the Commission of Inquiry's report this afternoon.

DONNY: Thank you, too. It's good to be back.

For the full text of the interim report on the disaster visit www.eleanorupdale.com/minute, where you will also find an archive of Radio Heathshire and newspaper reports on the disaster, tributes to many of the victims, and other material relating to the events of 16 December 2011.

THE VICTIMS OF THE HEATHWICK DISASTER

Most of the sixty-five who died were killed by falling masonry, flying glass, blast injuries and burns.

ON THE COACH:

Apley, Philip	56	Driver
Hunter, Elizabeth	36	Teacher
Johnson, Joshua	13	Child
Knight, Chenelle	12	Child
Kohli, Shilpa	13	Child
Lennahan, Rory	12	Child
Nailor, Calum	12	Child
Nandi, Rahil	12	Child
Palmer, Kayleigh	12	Child
Quinn, Jeffrey	13	Child
Tracy, Liam	12	Child
Young, Charmaine	13	Child

IN THE NEWSAGENT'S:

Cahill, Anthea	54	Gardener
Cahill, Patricia	56	Gardener
Noble, Chloe	2	Child
Noble, Lucy	26	Mother
Patel, Touseef	62	Newsagent

IN THE STREET BETWEEN THE NEWSAGENT'S AND THE BANK:

Alderson, Gavin	39	Gas company foreman
Carter, Sharon	24	Political researcher
Donaldson, Alice	55	Died walking to the funeral, having left the public bus
Donaldson, Joseph	57	Died walking to the funeral, having left the public bus
Dunn, Serena	29	Died walking to the funeral, having left the public bus
Lee, Lorraine	37	Housewife
Lewis, PC Nigel	22	Police officer
Wilkins, Sarah	83	Pensioner
An unidentified man, known only as 'Matey'	?50	

IN THE FLAT ABOVE THE WEDDING SHOP:
Potts, Terry   33   Art teacher

IN THE FLAT ABOVE THE FLORIST'S SHOP:
Sharp, Margaret   78   Pensioner

IN THE STREET BETWEEN THE BANK AND
THE CHURCH:
Daintree, Kate   17   School student
Dougall, Gillie   44   Housewife
Flood, Edmund   62   Died walking to the
                               funeral, having left the
                               public bus
Inman, Richard   26   Cyclist
Krasinski,
Stanislaw   40   Motorcyclist
Krasinski, Nina   38   Pillion passenger
Nailor, Janine   47   Florist, daughter of Mrs
                               Sharp

OUTSIDE THE CHURCH:
Larkin, Matthew   72   Retired steeplejack
Whatmore, Ben   68   Pensioner

AT THE PETROL STATION:
Hardy, John   29   General trader
Oxley, Keith   31   Tanker driver
Perry, Charles   42   Taxi driver

OUTSIDE THE BAKERY:

Harman, Joseph   35   Baker
Rabane, Lotte   79   Retired actress

IN THE FLAT ABOVE THE BAKERY:

Harman, David   73   Retired baker

IN THE BAKERY:

Harman, Sheila   70   Retired teaching assistant

IN THE STREET BETWEEN THE BAKERY AND THE LAUNDERETTE:

Broadbrook, Paul   27   Designer
Fletcher, Deanna   25   Clerical worker
Pilbury, Frank   44   Funeral director
Robinson, Norbert   34   Postman

IN THE COFFEE SHOP:

Davis, Belinda   37   Archivist
Eames, Lily   2   Child
Lang, Nell   2   Child
Lang, Polly   2   Child
Morgan, Juliet   39   Sales executive
Orme, William   47   Architect
Sorley, Suzanne   38   Mother
Sorley, Max   3   Child

IN THE FLAT ABOVE THE SHOE SHOP:
Gilliard, Noel   51   Author

IN THE SHOE SHOP:
Gibbon, Raquel   32   Unemployed

IN THE FLAT ABOVE THE DANCE STUDIO:
An unidentified
woman   ?25

IN THE DANCE STUDIO:
Tate, Maggie   30   Fitness instructor

IN THE LAUNDERETTE:
Lorenzo, Marco   67   Proprietor
Lorenzo, Stefano   30   Son of the above

MOTORISTS WHO DIED IN THEIR CARS:
Lapsom, Barbara   62   Retired nurse
Thorpe, Sally   25   Beautician
Viner, Kelly   17   School student

Many casualties suffered injuries, some extremely severe. The most seriously hurt were Nicholas Birkham, 19 (a charity worker); Leonard Gibbon, 13 (whose mother died in the shoe shop); Robert Grey, 36 (hearse driver); Farouk Osman, 24 (student); Francine Palmer,

38 (whose daughter died on the school coach); and Samuel Riley, 18 (a member of staff at the coffee shop).

Remember, too, Lucy Noble's unborn baby, who would have been a brother for Chloe, and Donald Whyman, 59, whose body, on its way to his funeral, was severely mutilated by an explosive blast. One of the two horses pulling the hearse was killed outright. Because the funeral director died and the carriage driver was seriously injured, there was no one to say whether it was Dime or Dollar. The other horse was gravely hurt. A veterinary surgeon put him out of his misery at the earliest possible opportunity, which was three hours after the explosions.

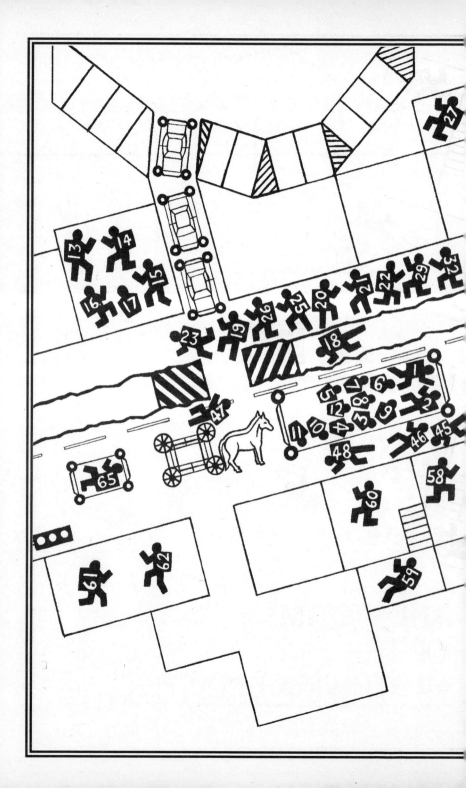

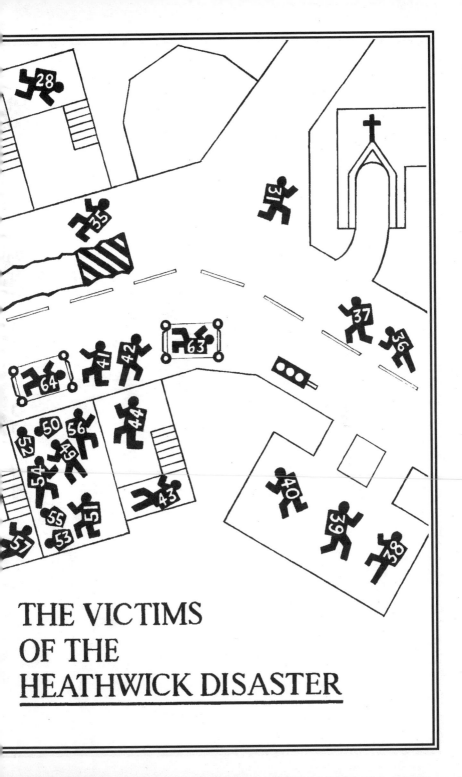

THE VICTIMS
OF THE
HEATHWICK DISASTER

KEY

1 Elizabeth Hunter
2 Philip Apley
3 Joshua Johnson
4 Chenelle Knight
5 Shilpa Kohli
6 Rory Lennahan
7 Calum Nailor
8 Rahil Nandi
9 Kayleigh Palmer
10 Jeffrey Quinn
11 Liam Tracy
12 Charmaine Young
13 Anthea Cahill
14 Patricia Cahill
15 Touseef Patel
16 Lucy Noble
17 Chloe Noble
18 Gavin Alderson
19 Lorraine Lee
20 Alice Donaldson
21 Joseph Donaldson
22 Serena Dunn
23 Sharon Carter
24 PC Lewis
25 Sarah Wilkins
26 Matey
27 Terry Potts
28 Margaret Sharp
29 Kate Daintree
30 Gillie Dougall
31 Edmund Flood
32 Richard Inman
33 Stanislaw Krasinski

34 Nina Krasinski
35 Janine Nailor
36 Matthew Larkin
37 Ben Whatmore
38 Keith Oxley
39 Charles Perry
40 John Hardy
41 Joseph Harman
42 Lotte Rabane
43 David Harman
44 Sheila Harman
45 Norbert Robinson
46 Paul Broadbrook
47 Frank Pilbury
48 Deanna Fletcher
49 Suzanne Sorley
50 Max Sorley
51 Belinda Davis
52 Lily Eames
53 Nell Lang
54 William Orme
55 Polly Lang
56 Juliet Morgan
57 Noel Gilliard
58 Raquel Gibbon
59 Unidentified woman
60 Maggie Tate
61 Marco Lorenzo
62 Stefano Lorenzo
63 Barbara Lapsom
64 Kelly Viner
65 Sally Thorpe